Claimed By Priest

Steel Order MC Series

Cassi Hart

Published by: Cheeky Publishing LLC

First Edition

Copyright © 2024 Cassi Hart– All rights Reserved.

All rights reserved. No part of this publication may be reproduced, stored in or introduced into a retrieval system, or transmitted, in any form, or by any means (electronic, mechanical, photocopying, recording, or otherwise) without the prior written permission of the copyright owner. The author acknowledges the trademarked status and trademark owners of various products referenced status and trademark owners of various products referenced in this work of fiction, which have been used without permission. The publication / use of the trademarks is not authorized, associated with or sponsored by the trademark owners. For any permission requests email cassi@cassihartromance.com

***

This is a work of fiction. Names, characters, places, and incidents either are products of the author's imagination or are used fictitiously. Any similarity to actual events or locales or persons, living or dead, is entirely coincidental.

Dedicated to my secret obsession with guys in leather and tattoos. Keep being amazing. Cheers!

Thank you for your support, enjoy!

Contents:

Chapter One 5

Chapter Two 19

Chapter Three 30

Chapter Four 40

Chapter Five 56

Chapter Six 70

Chapter Seven 85

Chapter Eight 101

Chapter Nine 113

Epilogue 128

About the Author 146

Chapter One

Sky

I'm lost.

A low groan slips out when I realize I have walked past the same coffee shop at least four times now. It's either that, or Austin has the same coffee shop on every block, with the same name and everything.

Something tells me it's the former.

Christ, this is not the time to suddenly lose my sense of direction. Not that there is ever a right time for that sort of thing, but this is definitely not it. As it turns out, I have been walking in circles. No clue how that would even happen since I've been following my phone's GPS, but here I am. Back at the same freaking coffee shop.

This feels like a horror movie where the actress keeps waking up to the same day and cannot move on until she finds a way to break the cycle.

Don't panic!

"You are not stuck in a movie, Sky. You're just a country girl visiting the city for the first time. I bet this has happened to everyone at some point in their lives," I reassure myself.

Long, deep breaths, Sky . . . slow and steady.

I tighten my fingers around my suitcases' handles and force myself not to hyperventilate, trying to figure out where I must have lost my way and why the heck I keep coming back to the same spot over and over again.

I can't keep doing this. It's getting late, and with the sun setting, I need to make sure I am off the streets and checked into my hotel before that happens. All the research I did prior to traveling suggested how unsafe the city is at night. An article I read a few days ago highlighted the nighttime muggings and other crimes done by the city's gangs terrorizing the people they catch outside in this part of town. A shudder races through my body just from the thought alone.

"This is what you get for leaving your little town behind and coming to the big city," a voice at the back of my head admonishes.

"No, this is my dream," I whisper firmly before doubt can take root in my thoughts. Besides, it's too late to second guess myself now. I'm already in Austin, and there is nothing waiting for me back in Marfa.

I rest my back against the brick wall of the coffee shop, shifting my focus from my thoughts to my surroundings, and for the first time since stepping off the bus, I take in the city.

I've dreamed of this very moment all my life.

The moment I would leave behind my dusty little town and move to the big city with its bustling streets and towering skyscrapers that seem to touch the clouds. The air here smells of car exhaust and coffee, neon lights illuminating the evening and casting a vibrant glow on the city. Hell, even the sunset feels different . . . almost magical as the sun slowly disappears behind the tall buildings.

And no, I didn't hate my little town, but I have always wanted more than what I could get there. I wanted to wake up to something other than the same dusty little shops and the mom-and-pop diner that's been there for at least three generations. It's a tight-knit community with the most caring people in the world, but somehow, I didn't fit, especially after my grandmother died.

Nana and I used to talk about this moment all the time, and she'd urge me to go out into the world. She'd tell me all these fascinating stories of her time in the city before she moved to our little town to marry my grandfather and have her happily ever after.

"You need to see the world, Sky. You're not going to find it in this little town."

Well, I'm here now. This is the dream we always talked about.

A smile graces my lips as a sense of calm settles in. It's the first semblance of peace I have felt since arriving in Austin, and I revel in it.

"See, it's not all bad," I whisper to myself, my eyes sweeping over my surroundings, and when my gaze settles on a group of teens leaning against the building across the street, chatting among themselves, my smile grows softer. The teens remind me of the kids back home with their messy hair and clothes. It seems the city and country kids all share the same brain when it comes to what they consider fashion. I bet their minds are wired the same...

Wait—

I straighten up in excitement as an idea settles in. I bet these kids are no different from the ones back home. The teens back home always jump in when you need help; I am certain I can ask these kids for help. My heart flutters with excitement as I pick up my bags before starting toward the boys.

There is a sunny smile on my face as I drag my suitcases behind me, watching for the traffic when I cross the road. I catch the boy's attention, and they briefly stop talking to watch me make my way to them. They say something among themselves before two of them break from the group and approach me with kind smiles on their faces. They look to be about high school age, and that puts me at ease.

"Ma'am," the taller of the two says kindly with a smile that I am sure charms all the girls in his neighborhood. "Do you need help?"

"Please," I sigh, relief clear in my voice. "Would you be kind enough to show me the way to Congress Avenue? I'm a little lost."

"Of course, it's just a few blocks from here," the other kid says with a smile equally as charming. "We'll take you there if you want. Those bags look heavy, can we help you carry them?"

My heart swells with warmth at the offer. These kids are indeed just like the ones from my hometown, always willing to offer a hand when needed.

I let them take the suitcases from my hands, as well my heavy backpack, groaning in relief when the weight drops from my shoulders. Those bags contain all my worldly possessions, so it makes sense they feel like they're full of bricks.

"Follow us," the taller kid says, and starts walking in the opposite direction the GPS kept sending me. I smile as I follow them down the street, taking in the massive buildings in fascination and thinking of all the exciting things I am going to do once I get settled in.

Austin is known for its historical landmarks, and the fact that it's famous for being the live music capital of the world only makes me want to start exploring immediately. I have all the time in the world to do that once I settle down and finish my college registration. I bet the boys know all the best spots to visit.

"What places would you guys recommend visiting?" I ask, shifting my eyes from the massive buildings to the boy walking beside me, except I am met by an unfamiliar face. I offer an apologetic smile before looking around for the boys carrying my bags, but I only see one unfamiliar face after another.

Oh God! Did I lose them in the crowd?

I palm my forehead with a chuckle. I couldn't look any more like a country bumpkin if I tried. I must've been so lost in my own world that I wandered away from them. They must have taken a turn or something, and I missed it. I rush forward, but find myself faced with a dilemma when I reach an intersection and still can't see the boys.

Christ, which way did they go?

I bite into my lower lip, straining my brain, but this is a puzzle I am not going to solve any time soon, and the longer I wait, the harder it'll be to catch up with them.

I turn around to ask for directions, but it seems no one is willing to stop and speak with me as they all seem to have somewhere to be, but when an older lady finally stops, she points not at one of the streets in the intersection, but behind us.

"Congress Avenue is several blocks that way," she says pointing the way I just came. "You must've missed it."

No, that can't be right.

The boys . . . They said . . .

A wave of exhaustion settles in as I try to make sense of what's happening. Did the older lady perhaps get it wrong? That has got to be it because the boys seemed confident this was the right direction.

There seems to be some sort of misunderstanding here, and I refuse to entertain any negative thoughts that try to creep in.

This . . . all of this is just a misunderstanding.

Slow deep breaths . . .

I sold everything I own and used all my savings and my small inheritance from my grandmother to come here, and now . . .

No!

I shake my head and run my trembling fingers through my hair as the possibility that the boys might've robbed me creeps in.

A hysterical laugh bubbles up my throat as the scary thought registers, but I refuse to let it stay.

No way, I think with a panicked chuckle. There is no way I was gullible enough to have gotten myself in trouble only a few hours into coming to the city.

"There is just no way!" I whisper, turning on my heels and running back to the spot where I first met the boys. I'll just find their friends, who can certainly help me get hold of my helpers, and everything will be fine.

Except nothing is fine.

Neither the boys nor their friends are in the spot I found them earlier, and it fully settles in that I let myself get robbed. Hell, I literally handed them my bags with everything from my clothes to my college forms, cash, ID, and credit card inside.

"Oh God," I whisper, the tremble in my knees threatening to send me to the ground, but I force myself to stay up.

Breathe, Sky!

Christ, it's much harder telling myself to breathe when my lungs feel like they're collapsing. I should have followed my grandmother's advice to never trust anyone I don't know in the city, but those boys... They were so nice and kind.

They seemed harmless.

With a shaky sigh, I pull my phone from the back pocket of my jeans and look up the closest police department. As with my GPS app, the data connection doesn't work, and I have to go into the nearest café and connect to the free internet. The closest police station doesn't seem to be far from my current location. Of course, I still manage to lose my way several times before finding it. I am greeted by a bored-looking man in his mid to late forties, who looks as interested in my story as one would be in watching paint dry.

"So, let me get this straight," he says with a barely suppressed yawn. "You arrive in the city and blindly trust a bunch of strangers to carry all of your bags and then act surprised when they run away with them?"

I bite into my lip and look down before nodding meekly. "Yes."

"Miss," he drawls lazily. "Why would you trust a bunch of kids you have never met?"

Why wouldn't I?

Do I need to look at everyone with suspicion? Is that the mentality I need to adopt for life in the city?

"T-they seemed like nice kids," I offer weakly.

In hindsight, I can see how much of a mistake that was, but in my town, something like this would never happen. The teenage boys would have gladly helped me carry my luggage with a charming smile before running off.

Everything is different here.

The people here frown when you smile at them, and the cops look at you with annoyance when you walk into their station. Hell, no one even stops to ask what's wrong when they see you distressed.

You wanted this, my conscience admonishes again. *To be another faceless body in the crowd.*

"This is what will happen, Miss Tyler," the officer says with a sigh, one of many he's let out since I walked in. "We are going to investigate and let you know if we come up with something, but in cases like this, it's pretty hard to recover anything."

"I can buy new clothes and shoes; I already called to cancel my cards. I don't care about those things, but my personal records, school forms, letter of admission, and ID are all in my backpack. I need them to register for my classes."

"Like I said, we'll look into that and get back to you," he says. "Write down your contact information and an address where we can reach you."

I grab the pen he hands me and gnaw at my lip as I try to think of what to do. I don't exactly have an address to note down. I was going to stay at a hotel for the night and report to college tomorrow where I would get a dorm assignment, but now, without any documentation or means to pay for a room, that's not going to happen.

"What's the matter?"

I lift my eyes to the officer. "I'm sorry, but I don't have an address to note down. I'll have one tomorrow when I can get moved into my dorm, but I was planning to stay at a hotel tonight."

The cop studies me for a long time before grabbing a notebook and scribbling something down. He tears the paper off the notebook and passes it over to me.

"This is the address to a women's shelter," he tells me. "Just tell them that Officer Rowling sent you, and they will take you in for a few nights. I'll let you know if we find your things."

"Thank you," I say, getting up to leave, but the cop stops me, his eyes flashing with something dangerous, but it's gone so fast I almost think I've imagined it.

"A pretty girl such as yourself should not be walking around this dangerous city. You'll be safest at the shelter."

I grow a little self-conscious when he runs his eyes over my body, so I thank him and quickly exit the station before he or anyone else can see the tears in my eyes. Tear droplets fall on the screen of my phone as I search for the address to the women's shelter, and want to cry when I see it's a thirty-minute walk. At night. I don't have the means to pay for an Uber or taxi. For the first time since coming to the city, I entertain the thought that perhaps I have been chasing a pipe dream.

The city is nothing like I imagined. When Nana told me to go out into the world, she didn't prepare me for how miserable the world would leave me feeling.

And just how lonely.

Chapter Two

Priest

There have been few occasions in my life when I have felt the will to live start to slip right through my fingers, but the need has never been as intense as it is right now.

Fucking hell!

My fingers are practically itching to grab my gun from the holster and shoot my brains out if only to escape this torture.

"I'm telling you, man, nothing beats the roar of a Harley with a straight-pipe exhaust. It's all about that deep, thunderous sound that turns heads everywhere you go. Don't listen to anyone who tells you otherwise," Knight, my best friend and also the vice president of our motorcycle club, says, smacking the kid sitting beside him on the back of his head.

The prospect, who is in his early twenties, shakes his head. "Dude, I hear you, but I gotta disagree. It's not about the noise and the power; it's all about the looks. Adding chrome accents and custom paint jobs can take a Harley to a whole new level." The kid turns to his flashy bike with a fond smile. "What's the point of turning heads with all the noise without giving them something to look at?"

I close my eyes and beg for patience to survive the night. These two have been going at it all night long, and I am just about ready to start my Harley and ride off the edge of the nearest cliff so I can put an end to it.

"You're both wrong!"

I fight a groan when a voice comes from my left, and I don't have to look to see Reaper's stoic face boring holes into the side of my head. My enforcer has been an otherwise silent observer to the squabble between my VP and the prospect, so I'm confused why he would even want to join in and add to the headache.

"Comfort is key for a Harley," he says. "A well-padded seat and handlebars can make those long rides a breeze. It's all about finding that sweet spot between style, power, and comfort. What do you think, Prez?

Kill me, is what I am think.

"I think I should have come on this stakeout alone tonight," I say roughly, digging my hand into my jacket and coming out with a pack of cigarettes. I grab one and slip it between my lips before lighting it and taking a long drag of nicotine.

"I thought you quit smoking," Knight says, his eyes narrowed on me.

"I did," I deadpan, taking another long pull of the cigarette. The truth is that I tried to quit the nasty habit, and no, it's not because I am thinking of my health and all that crap. I am not delusional enough to think I am going to live long enough to worry about the long-term effects of smoking.

Not in this business, I won't.

Between the trigger-happy cops and our careless rival MCs in the area, it'll be a miracle if I make it to fifty without a bullet in my head or a lifetime sentence to my name like my old man.

The reason I've tried to quit my nasty smoking habit is because that's all it is, a habit. I am not fond of being a slave to my habits. I've seen enough people go bat shit crazy from substance abuse to know I need my head screwed on straight. I can't afford any compulsions, and my smoking is exactly that. I've managed to stay off anything that controls my head and even gone for months without smoking, and yet . . .

And yet, I can't quit because of these meatheads.

"I see just how hard you're trying to quit," Knight says, sarcasm dripping off him like honey, and he's lucky he's my best friend, or he would be on the ground bleeding right now. He must read the dangerous glint in my eyes because he quickly changes the topic. "What are we doing here anyway? We should—"

His words are cut off when we all catch the sound of a distant truck. Everyone goes alert and checks their weapons as the truck gets closer.

"Fucking finally!" I hiss, blowing out smoke before dropping the cigarette to the ground and putting it out with the heel of my boot.

We've been waiting for this truck all night. A few days ago, when a prospect reported spotting trucks traveling through a secluded part of our territory, I immediately knew who it belonged to. Only the Black Chains MC would be brave enough to transport drugs through our territory. The only other route into the city is by the highway, but they risk getting caught by the State Highway Patrol that way. We've been hanging out for the past two nights waiting for them to show up again, and they just did.

Tonight, I intend to remind these fuckers why the authorities are the safer choice in comparison to us.

"How hard do we go on them?" Reaper asks quietly at my side, and I watch as my enforcer pulls out a silencer. I can practically see him drooling at the thought of the violence that is about to ensue.

"As hard as you need to," I say, taking out my own gun. "We will teach them a lesson tonight!"

I nod at Knight, who will ride after Reaper and me with the prospect. The plan is for those two to attack from the back in case there are men hiding there, and for Reaper and me to deal with the men at the front.

We break off as previously discussed to ambush the truck, and everything happens in a flash. My gun is already drawn as I ride my Harley to the front of the truck, momentary distracting the driver from Reaper, who shoots the tire, forcing it to a stop.

Then bullets start flying.

The Black Chains were clearly underprepared for this ambush, and we quickly subdue them, dragging three bleeding men from the truck who plead with us not to kill them. Despite my words to Reaper earlier, I don't plan on killing them. At least not all three of them. I still need someone to take a message back to the Black Chains.

I am not as bloodthirsty as some of my crew members. Someone has to be sane enough to lead this pack of animals, and unfortunately, that's me. Even so, I need to teach these fuckers a lesson about what it means to cross the president of the Steal Order MC.

I point my gun at the man closest to me, ready to pull the trigger, when Knight's voice stops me.

"Hey, Priest, you need to see this!" His voice is rough and cold, but that's not what stops me. Knight and the rest of the members rarely call me by name unless it's serious. I am always Prez to them, the cold man with a permanent scowl and a dead heart.

"Shoot if anyone moves a muscle." I nod to Reaper before walking around the truck to the back. I expect to find tons of cocaine loaded in the back, or perhaps weapons, but what I am met with has my blood chilling in my veins. "What the fuck is this!"

"I knew the Black Chains were the scummiest of the scum, but this is downright disgusting!"

A whimpering noise from inside the truck sets my jaw in a tight grind as I stare at the girls huddled together in the corner. Knight flashes a light over the small spaces, and I mentally count the number of the people in the truck to ten girls, most of whom don't even look old enough to drive.

"W-what are we going to do?" the prospect asks shakily, his eyes wide with horror as it slowly dawns on him that we've stopped human trafficking.

"Call in a tip to our contact at the sheriff's office," I tell him. "Inform him that he needs to get out here ASAP with his friends from social services."

Despite our love-hate relationship with law enforcement, we've found ourselves in situations where we have had to tip them off when we aren't in a position to deal with something, but those occasions are few and far between and we always go through the same contact, the only man in uniform I'm willing to trust.

This truck filled with terrified women is clearly not something we can deal with. Most of them look underage . . . We don't have the resources to sort this out and get these girls home.

The prospect disappears to make the call, leaving me alone with Knight. I turn to him to instruct him to load the Black Chains into the SUV Reaper drove out here for this purpose. We'll deal with these men ourselves and get all the information we can from them. It doesn't really matter what the girls tell the police happened to them. The cops won't care enough to track down three low-level grunts, and there will be no proof we were ever here.

Knight nods and walks away, and I don't realize until he's gone that he's left me with a bunch of terrified girls.

Built like a tank, I am a six-foot-three giant with a face that's been said to give kids nightmares. I have a deep rumbly voice and would have these girls screaming at the top of their lungs if I dared try to comfort them.

Not that I would know what to say anyway.

Shit!

My fingers itch with the need to reach into my jacket and take out a cigarette, but I stop myself before I can do that. The only other option is to stand awkwardly outside the truck with my massive build blocking most of the moonlight.

Fuck! Maybe I shouldn't have sent Knight away. He always seems to attract women to him with his good looks and charming words. Hell, even Reaper would do better in my position.

"Jesus Christ! What is taking so long!" I hiss under my breath, unsure what to do but unwilling to leave the girls alone. Realistically, I know it's impossible for the cops to get here anywhere under twenty minutes considering how far our territory is from the city, but that doesn't exactly calm me down.

We have to time our departure with their arrival just right so we aren't caught up with the police ourselves.

I am so tightly strung and distracted that I don't hear one of the girls climb out of the back of the truck until someone taps my shoulder, startling me.

I whip around quickly, my breath catching in my throat when my eyes lock with clear baby blue ones that remind me of the sky on a calm day. The girl, about a foot or so shorter than me, stares up at me with teary eyes that cause a rumbling growl at the back of my throat.

Christ, even with her mussed-up golden hair and tear-streaked cheeks, she seems like an angel. Everything about her, from the way she watches me to the air about her, catches me off guard and renders me speechless. All I can do is . . . stare.

"A-are you—" She cuts herself off to clear her voice, which comes out a little husky. "Are you here to save us?"

I open my lips to say something, but my thoughts can't seem to settle on what exactly I need to say with her watching me the way she is . . . So, I simply nod.

Her eyes well up with tears again, and I have to stop myself from stepping forward to make it right. For the first time in my life, I wish I was Knight. My best friend would know the right thing to say to comfort her.

He would know what to do and—

"Oh!" I gasp when the girl flings herself into my arms, wrapping her hands around my shoulders and burying her face against my chest before breaking into a heart-wrenching sob.

"Thank you," she sniffs into my shirt. "You have no idea how scared we've been. Thank you."

My hands remain by my sides, confused by the girl's reaction and unsure how to respond.

No one besides my sister has hugged me in years, and never like this.

Nothing this warm. Nothing this devastating.

This girl . . . wrecks me to the core.

Chapter Three

Sky

He smells of cigarettes and leather.

I never imagined I would cling to a scent like a lifeline, bury myself against steel-hard muscles, and want to forget . . .

Forget about the last twenty-four hours of hell.

I tighten my hands around the man's shoulders to stifle my cry, and I know it should mortify me just how tightly I am clinging to this stranger, but . . . I can't help myself. This is the first time in what feels like days I have felt any semblance of peace.

After what I've been through, I don't have it in me to be mortified.

"Hey Prez, our contact said they'll be here in fifteen," someone calls from behind me, and I know . . . I realize I should snap out of whatever's gotten into me and withdraw from the embrace, but I can't get my body to move away from this giant of a man.

A shiver shakes my body when he lifts a massive palm to my head to cup it, and I let his awkward pats soothe and ground me.

"Thank you for rescuing us," I whisper again, losing myself in the stranger's scent.

When the police officer I'd given my report to stopped me a couple blocks down the street to offer me a ride to the women's shelter, I'd eagerly accepted. I'd always believed that the police could be trusted implicitly. I've now learned how very wrong I was. Despite my best efforts, I'd quickly fallen asleep in the patrol car, lulled by a sense of safety after a stressful day.

I'd woken to the sound of gravel crunching under tires as we pulled into a field. Before I could ask where we were or what was happening, I was abruptly pulled from the car and thrown into the back of a box truck by men whose faces I couldn't see. I thought it was the end of my life. I figured I was being kidnapped, so I tried to plead with them to let me go, telling them that I had no money or family to pay my ransom, but they simply shoved a gun to my temple and threatened to shoot me if I made a sound.

It wasn't until I saw the other girls in the truck that I realized I wasn't being kidnapped for ransom.

What were the chances that I would get trafficked within only a few hours of being robbed of all my possessions? How could I be so unlucky?

"You're okay," the beast rumbles in my ear, sending a tremor down my neck and calming me further.

He saved me. I remind myself that this beast of a man and his friends saved us. I am not delusional enough to think they're the good guys. Not with their cold, hard eyes and tattooed arms and necks. But in this moment, they're our heroes.

The thought drives home the knowledge that a person's trustworthiness can never be judged on appearances alone.

A bunch of baby-faced teens robbed me, and a tired, middle-aged cop facilitated my being trafficked, along with a bunch of other girls. After my panic-riddled brain calmed down a bit and I realized that, at nineteen, I was the oldest among the kidnapped girls, I tried to be strong. I promised the sobbing girls that someone would come for us even though I hadn't believed it myself.

I tried not to show how badly this city had beaten me in only a few hours.

Christ, I'm so tired!

I burrow deeper into the giant's arms when I realize I don't need to be strong anymore and don't pull away until I hear one of the girls sniffle back a sob. Only then do I force myself away from the solid embrace and turn back to the truck, ignoring the tears that drip down my cheeks.

"You can come out, girls," I call out. "The police are on their way. We're safe now."

They hesitate, but only for a second before they all start filing out, one after the other. Most of the girls are underage and were kidnapped right off the streets after running away from home or in a similar fashion as me.

I push back my feelings and comfort the girls, hugging the youngest one until someone announces that the cops are only a few minutes out. The giant of a man turns toward me.

"That's my cue. The police will be here any minute. They'll take care of you. We were never here, do you understand?"

"What?" I cry. "No! You can't leave." I don't know how to put into words how terrified I am at the thought of this man leaving.

My tone must frighten the small girl in my arms because she whimpers and clings to me tighter. I give her a squeeze before passing her off to the girl next to me, who appears to be only a couple of years older than her. Fortunately, she goes willingly, and I am able to turn back to the man. Only to find he's walking away.

"Hey! Wait!" I shout, chasing after him. I rush to his side and put a hand on his arm, causing him to whirl around quickly. His eyes have a dangerous glint to them, and I gasp, backing up so fast, I nearly fall over my feet. He reaches out quickly and grabs my arms to steady me.

"Are you okay?" His eyes soften as they meet mine, and I realize he isn't as scary as I'd first believed. I think his friend called him Priest. Not sure if that's his real name or his profession, but either way, those dark eyes threaten to undo what little control I am clinging to.

I hold back from jumping into his arms this time, despite how badly I want to.

"I'm . . ." I start to assure him that I am fine, but I would be lying. I'm the furthest thing from okay, but that doesn't matter now. "The police . . . It was a cop that kidnapped me. How do we know these police are safe? That we'll be okay? Can't you stay with us?" I'm babbling, I know, but the thought of this man leaving me behind has icy dread coursing through my veins.

Priest's eyes go dangerously dark again, and he clenches his jaw. Somehow, though, I know his anger isn't directed at me. "They're safe, I promise you. They will make sure everyone gets the care they need and is reunited with their families."

"How can you be so sure?" I whisper, staring into the giant's coal black eyes, so dark they threaten to suck me into their bottomless depths, but I refuse to look away. I need this—to know that the girls are safe is the only thing keeping me standing at this point.

Priest studies me for a moment, his gaze sending a rush of heat down my spine. "I have connections on the force. I will follow up to make sure the girls are united with their families."

I believe him. I don't have the best track record for trusting people, but I trust this man for some reason.

I breathe out a relieved sigh. "Thank you. But, um, what about the girls who don't have family?"

Dark eyes narrow on me once more, and out of the corner of my eye, I can see flashing lights across the barren distance.

"C'mon, Prez, we have to go!" a man on a large, dark motorcycle shouts. Priest waves him off.

"Go on. I'll be right behind you." To me, he asks, "Which of the girls doesn't have family to go home to?"

From our time locked in the truck together, I know that I am actually the only one of us who doesn't have a home or family waiting for me. I gulp, trying to force back the trembling that's overtaken my body, then answer, "M-me. I, um, don't have anyone . . ."

Priest looks at me for a beat then over his shoulder at the quickly approaching lights. He curses under his breath, then takes my hand and leads me over to his bike. "I can't be here when the police arrive, but I can't leave you on your own either. You can come with me, and we'll figure out what to do."

A cry erupts from behind us, and I turn to see the young girl who'd hugged me rip herself away from the other girl and run toward me. "Where are you going? He can't take you!" she says on a sob when she reaches me, throwing her small arms around my waist.

I grip her shoulders tightly and look back at Priest, who nods, then I turn back to the girl. "It's okay, sweetheart," I soothe. "The police are coming—the *real* police, men and women who will protect you and make sure you get home. You're safe now, I promise." It's not a vow I should be making, but something tells me it's the truth. "I don't have a family waiting for me. Pr—" I cut myself off, realizing abruptly that he probably doesn't want any of us to know his name. "This man is going to help me. I'll be okay."

The young girl sniffles, but she lets me go and returns to the others, who are huddled close together next to the box truck.

With one last look at them as the lights of the police cars draw closer, I turn and join Priest next to his bike. He helps me put on a helmet, then before he gets on the bike, he slings his leather jacket over my shoulders. It smells strongly of him, the mix of leather and cigarettes oddly comforting. I didn't realize how cold I am until now.

"Thank you," I whisper, burrowing deeper into its warmth.

"Where do you want to go?" Priest asks as he helps me settle on the bike behind him. His touch on my arm is warm and reassuring even through the thick material of his jacket.

"Can you take me back twenty-four hours before I came to Austin?" I joke, but really, there is nothing funny about this situation.

"I can take you to a gated compound with more than twenty bikers living there—most of whom are fully armed—and offer you a room where you can sleep without having to worry about your safety."

Sleep. Comfort. Peace.

They all sound like such foreign concepts, and yet, I crave them more than I do my next breath.

I tug the leather jacket closer, letting his scent calm me before looking up to his face. "Will you be there?" I ask him, my voice breaking as I try to search his eyes in the dark. "Will you stay with me?"

It's crazy. After everything that's happened today, perhaps what I need is a room with at least three locks and the dresser pressed against the door . . .

No! What I need is a strong presence to fight off all the demons that threaten to pull me under. I don't want to be alone. Not tonight.

"I'll stay with you."

Chapter Four

Priest

I thought quitting cigarettes was difficult, but getting any sleep in bed with a girl wrapped around me like a damn octopus is impossible.

I've been up for hours—and hard for just as long—which makes me feel like the most perverted bastard alive. After everything that's happened to this girl, the last thing she needs is for the guy she expects to protect her to be sporting a hard on, but . . . I can't help it.

It's been a long night.

When we pulled up at the compound, Reaper and Knight were already in the Barn with the three Black Chains we'd grabbed tonight, and I wanted to join them there and extract information from the men myself, but one look at the bright-eyed girl in my arms, and I knew there would be no leaving her.

Sky refused my offer to take any one of the empty rooms I'd shown her, adamant about staying with me.

Since when do I freaking give in to anyone? I am the president of the Steel Order MC. The man the cops are terrified to approach and whose name is enough to have most people's blood freezing in their veins, and yet, all it takes to undo me is a pair of blue eyes.

Pathetic.

To think that this is what brings me to my knees is truly ridiculous, but I can't help it . . . or even hate it.

What I do hate, however, is the fact that all I can do is look at her. I can't touch her, no more than I am doing right now, or I will be damned for sure.

The girl is nineteen, for fuck's sake—more than a decade younger than me should be all it takes to discipline my mind and body into behaving, but there's no convincing my body of that with her perfect one pressed hard against mine, and Christ . . . she's so soft.

It was the first thing I noticed when she climbed into bed and attached herself to my side before immediately falling asleep.

I clench and unclench my fist as I try to shift under her, so her thigh is not pressed so close to my raging erection, but the move has her clinging tighter, and I have to bite back a groan at the pleasure that shoots up my spine. My eyes shoot to the alarm clock, and I groan when I realize it's only three in the morning. Unless I am willing to leave the bed entirely and risk waking the clearly exhausted girl, I'll have to bear it.

This is truly a test of my control.

"Am I too heavy?" A soft sultry voice breaks through the otherwise silent room, shocking me. "I'm sorry for lying down like this, but it's just so cold and your body is a furnace."

Fuck, does that mean she can feel my erection pressed up against her?

"I thought you were asleep," I say, clenching my teeth against another groan when the temptress moves up a bit, brushing her thigh against my hard cock.

"I can't sleep," she whispers. "Every time I close my eyes, I see the masked men grab me from the police car and shove a gun against my head, threatening to shoot me if I made a noise."

My jaw clenches harder at her words, the need to punish the men in the Barn growing by the second, but a logical part reminds me there are more people involved in the scheme. "You're safe now," I promise.

Long seconds tick by before she props herself up on an elbow and looks down at me, her eyes meeting mine in the dimly lit room. It's light enough to see her clearly though, since she'd shyly asked me to leave the en suite bathroom's light on before we climbed into bed. Given everything she's been through, I can understand why she'd be afraid of the dark now, and I was happy to grant her request.

Her eyes are a mesmerizing shade of blue. I'd thought so when I first saw her, and with her so close, I can read the innocence in them that slowly undoes me. She brings out a protective side I never knew I had.

A side that wants to bask in that innocence and protect it from the rest of the world.

The Black Chains came so close to shattering that innocence in her eyes, and my blood boils just thinking about it.

"You're the first decent bad guy I've met since coming to Austin," she whispers, breaking into a laugh when my brows draw in confusion. The sound she lets out is light and airy, and it sends my heart tugging with longing, and I realize I would do anything to hear it every day. "Nana always told me not to judge a book by the cover, but I never believed her until I came here. Thank you for saving my life, Priest."

Sky leans down and brushes her lips to the side of my mouth. It's nothing more than a touch of skin, but it sends my heart thumping in my chest and cock leaking in my sweats.

I want her!

She must feel my cock move—what with it pressed against her thigh—because her eyes widen with a look of wonder. I know she reads the desire written on my face as her cheeks slowly darken to a pretty rosy tinge.

She bites into her lips, and her eyes dart down to my mouth before meeting mine again. That is all it takes to snap at my control. I bring my hand to her hair and wrap her long golden waves around my fist. Her lips part on a gasp when I tug lightly at her hair, all the while watching for her reaction under my heated gaze.

"If you want to thank me with a kiss, then let me show you how I like it."

Her chest rises and falls quickly, pushing her perfect tits against my pecs, causing a harsh throb in my cock. I bring my free hand to her ass and shift her over me, so my erection is between her legs, and . . . I give her a moment to protest, to push me away, but her pretty blue gaze stays on mine. Her perfect eyes grow dazed when I rock my hard cock against her cloth-covered sex, fighting with everything I have not to shoot in my sweatpants.

She'd taken a shower when we'd gotten to my room, it was the only time she'd let me out of her sight for more than a few minutes. Now she's wearing one of my old T-shirts and a pair of my boxers. It'd be so easy to strip her bare.

When I bring my lips up to meet hers, her eyes flutter to a close.

"Priest," she whimpers against my lips, her breath coming in short pants.

Mine! comes the unbidden thought.

I've never thought of a woman in this way before. Sure, I've enjoyed their company, but it never crossed my mind to keep them longer than a few hours. As the president of the biggest motorcycle club in Austin, I already have too much on my plate to bother with entertaining women, but with Sky . . . I can't imagine not having her watching me the way she is right now. Like the sun and the moon hang over my head.

I can't imagine her looking at any other guy this way.

Fuck it!

With a harsh groan, I press my lips hard against hers, urging her to open up for me. I tug at her hair, which makes her lips part for my tongue, and fucking hell, she tastes like heaven. It's intoxicating. She whimpers as she shyly gives into my advances, opening up more for me as I slide our tongues together in a wet hungry kiss. Soon, I am drunk from the taste and warm texture of her lips.

My heart hammers as I devour her sexy little mouth, and when she starts writhing and mewling with her body rocking against my throbbing cock, she threatens to push me to the edge.

It's tempting . . . so fucking tempting to tear off the clothes standing in the way between my cock and her sexy little cunt, drive into her warmth, and spend the entire night buried inside her. Christ, I want to palm those perfect tits pressed up against me, take the little rosy buds into my mouth, and suck until the whole clubhouse hears her, but . . . I don't want to scare her. Not when I am practically dripping with the need to fuck her.

She can't handle me, not like this.

Not when my body is vibrating with the need to slam her smaller body to the mattress and rut her like a sex-starved beast.

I dig my hands into her ass to stop her grinding against my erection before breaking the kiss. She whines when I stop her movement, her dazed eyes locking with mine in a fever of heat. Her eyes are soft and needy, staring down at me like I have just unlocked something in her.

"You need rest," I say roughly, trying to be the kind of guy she mentioned earlier and not jump her after the traumatic night she's had, but she's having none of it.

"No, I need this," she tells me, licking at her swollen lips, and fuck... the things that tongue does to me. "I... Can you let me have this? Please?"

Fucking hell!

I join our lips again, and this time, I don't need to coax her into opening for me as she moans into the kiss. Her hips are restless as she rocks against my hardness, her movements growing fevered when I slip my hand under the shirt and palm her ass.

I shouldn't be doing this.

This is wrong. To want her the way I do is wrong, I know that, and yet, I can't stop. Not when she responds so needily to my touch.

When she begs so prettily, how can I say no to her?

"Fuck" I curse at my nonexistent control, equally hating and loving just how weak my pretty little stranger leaves me feeling.

With a rough growl, I flip us so she's lying on her back before dropping my lips to her jaw, running my hungry mouth behind her ear, and biting at the sensitive skin. She's panting roughly as I kiss a trail down her neck, nipping at the skin and soothing it with my tongue.

My head is buried in her neck, licking at the smooth column of her throat even as my fingers close around the waistband of her borrowed boxers and yank them down before tearing them completely off her. I toss them aside even as I start the slow descent down her body.

"Priest . . . I . . . Oh, God!" Her back arches off the bed with a cry when I drag my tongue over her nipples through the shirt. I lift my hand to her tits, pinching a small bud through the shirt as I suck at the other, my cock threatening to bust from the need that shoots up my spine.

I need to feel her. I thought this would be enough, but there is no holding back.

Gripping the shirt at the collar, I tear it in two, the sound loud in the room as my eyes fall on her perfect little globes with rosy peaks begging for my touch.

Mine!

"Beautiful," I rasp thickly, leaning down to lick at her puckered bud, and she cries out when my mouth closes hotly around it. I circle my tongue over the pebbled nipple, losing myself in her soft velvety skin. "You have no idea how much I fucking want you, princess."

I lift my eyes to lock with hers, and I am surprised to find them heated with need. "Princess?" she asks, her voice low and sultry, shooting straight to my balls.

"You don't like it?"

I pinch her nipple between my knuckles and tug lightly, watching through lust-clouded lenses as her lips part in a gasp and her eyes roll back. The way she reacts . . . it's so raw. It's as if no one has touched her before, but that can't be true. There is no way someone as gorgeous as this girl has not been touched before, but the thought of Sky being a virgin sends a pulse drumming in my throat.

"I like it," she whispers, snapping back into the present. "No one's ever called me that before. No one's ever touched or kissed me the way you do."

"How far have you gone before?" *How much of me can you take tonight?*

She bites her lips, driving me to the point of insanity with that simple move. "Nothing . . . I wanted to wait." Her eyes shift away from me, but only for a second, and when they lock on mine again, I read the resolution in her gaze before she can voice it. "I don't want to wait any longer."

My eyes stay locked on hers as I draw a hand up her thigh, parting her legs and stroking her feminine lips with my middle finger to part her folds. Her body shudders visibly as I rub my thumb in circles over her drenched pussy. "Are you sure about this, princess?"

"Yes," she pants.

"If you let me go further than this, no one else is allowed to touch you." My voice is firm as I drag my knuckle up her pussy. "Tell me you understand."

She nods eagerly, it would be comical if my own dick wasn't threatening to tear holes in my sweatpants.

I kiss a trail down her body before settling between her parted thighs. I grab her leg and rest it on my shoulders before she can hide herself, exposing her sex further. My mouth is drooling when my eyes lock with her untouched pussy, and good heaven, she's perfect. I slide my hands under her thighs and clutch her ass, drawing her closer to me, and nothing could have prepared me for the intoxicating peachy scent that hits me. I'm a starved man as I lean down and kiss her parted flesh with a needy groan. I give her little warning before going all in, sliding my tongue through her wet valley and lapping at her slick arousal.

"Fuck, princess," I breathe roughly against her trembling sex. "You're practically dripping for Daddy."

A shudder rocks her body, and it takes me a second to realize what I've just said. Jesus Christ, I have no idea where that came from. Sex has always been just a means to an end for me. I've never thought about it long enough to consider having a kink, and suddenly . . . this!

What have you done to me, Sky?

"Daddy," she mimics, her voice breathy, and from her lips, the words sound right.

Fuck!

I dig my fingers into her thighs before dropping my tongue back to her wet valley and bathing her clit in long fast strokes that send her arching off the bed with a sob.

"Say it again," I say harshly between licks, her intoxicating scent sending my head reeling and this—Sky—is all I can think about at the moment.

"Daddy!" she sobs brokenly even as her pussy begins to quiver, and I can tell she is close. I seal my lips over her smooth clit and suck gently at the swollen bud, drawing out a scream from her lips. She thrashes on the bed as her body trembles in beautiful spasms. "Oh, God . . . Daddy!" Her tits rise and fall so beautifully that I momentarily forget my throbbing cock, and instead, watch this beauty come apart in my arms.

Mine!

I lap at her drenched pussy until her body has stopped shaking and all that's left are tiny tremors. Her eyes are dazed when she looks down her body to lock them with mine. I slowly lower her leg from my shoulder and climb back up her body, even as I reach into my sweatpants for my cock.

I lick at the wetness sticking to my lips and stare down at the girl I intend to make mine completely, but not yet. Christ, it would be so easy to push my leaking cock into her tight, slick pussy and claim her, but I don't think I would last.

When I do fuck her, I intend to spend more than three seconds inside of her perfect body.

My skin flames when I feel soft hands join mine on my cock. I study Sky's flushed face as she takes my length into her much smaller and softer hands. "Let me help," she whispers shyly, and I do.

I lose myself in those perfect blues as she strokes my cock with clumsy hands, the knowledge that I am the only man she has ever touched makes my balls draw up tight with the need to come, and it doesn't take more than three strokes before I am erupting with a groan. I unload a hot endless stripe of white on her stomach and pussy. Her eyes stay intimately locked on mine as she milks me to the last drop, and when I lean down to claim her mouth, she opens up for me.

Perfect. The night gifted me the precious girl.

Mine!

My breathing is still labored when we break the kiss, and as much as I want to fall beside her, I need to clean us first. I brush my lips over hers before climbing out of bed and heading to the bathroom. When I come back with a wet towel, it's to find Sky already dozing.

I guess she meant it when she said she needed this.

I clean her up quickly and tuck her in. She doesn't stir or make a sound, and I clean up quickly before joining her in bed.

It's reckless, I know.

I know little to nothing about this girl the universe sent my way, but what I do know for sure is how hard she makes my heart beat and the protective feelings she brings stirs up in me. I would kill for her.

I guess that's all that matters.

Chapter Five

Sky

On my tenth birthday, the cops showed up at my middle school instead of one of my parents. I was terrified, knowing immediately that something was wrong.

Turns out I was right. My parents had gotten into an accident. After that, I'd gone to live with Nana, my father's mother. I loved my Nana dearly, and she'd been alone since my grandfather had passed away. And then she'd lost her only child. We took solace in each other over our shared grief.

Living with Nana was easy. She let me eat ice cream and baked an unhealthy number of cookies. She let me have my way, and I was extremely spoiled.

She was all I had, and when I lost her too, I never imagined I would ever experience those feelings of love and comfort with anyone ever again.

And yet, here I am, with a bowl of ice cream someone was forced to fetch for me.

When I woke up a little after noon, all the events of yesterday slammed into me hard and overshadowed the magical moment Priest and I had shared last night. I needed something sweet and familiar to comfort me, so I'd asked if there was any ice cream. If Priest thought my request was strange, he said nothing of it.

Half an hour later, someone showed up with a pint of mine and Nana's favorite cookie dough ice cream. Apparently, they hadn't had any ice cream at the clubhouse, and Priest had someone get it for me.

"Do you need anything else?" Priest asks from where he's seated watching me. "Tell me if you need anything, and I will send one of the boys to get it for you."

"I'm okay," I say, scooping ice cream into my mouth, and this time, when I say the words, I actually mean them.

I don't know if it's the ice cream, the heavily tattooed giant seated next to me on this porch, or a combination of the two, but I feel better already.

I break my gaze from Priest and look at my surroundings. I couldn't make out much when we arrived last night, but now, I take in the sights around me. There's a long, gated driveway that runs past the porch where I'm sitting before branching off to a few outbuildings. The area around the house and buildings is clear and well maintained, but the property itself is surrounded by dense woods. The house is massive, at least three stories. It has blue vinyl siding and a wraparound porch with several rocking chairs and a swing. The gardens look well-tended, and everything is surprisingly clean. It is nothing like what I would expect from a motorcycle club.

As I waited for my ice cream, Priest had explained that the house serves as the club's main hub, the clubhouse. Everyone in the club is free to come and go as they please. Patched-in members have the right to live in one of the house's many bedrooms, which are assigned based on seniority. As the club president, Priest has the master suite.

Those members with families, and whoever else chooses to, live in their own homes, leaving only the single and newest members living in the clubhouse for the most part. Prospects are required to live in the clubhouse for a full year and are responsible for maintaining the property.

On Wednesdays, all fifteen senior members of the club living in the area are required to attend Church, a meeting to discuss club business. Afterward, the entire club and their families, sometimes a hundred people or more, are invited to gather behind the clubhouse for a cookout, weather permitting.

Priest also explained to me that he has his own house where he lived with his younger sister. But since she left for college, he has been staying in his suite at the clubhouse, preferring to be in the center of things.

The outbuildings are bathed in sunlight, their vibrant red color standing out against the blue sky. As I look around, I notice security features here and there, like cameras and keypad locks, and it all blows my mind.

Perhaps I was expecting them to live in a rundown trailer park with grease-covered men walking around the space like I've seen in the movies, but this place is organized and efficient. There's something welcoming and homey about it too.

From a distance, I catch the sound of engines revving, and that sends a thrill rocking through my body. Before last night, I'd never been on a motorcycle, and now, I wonder if Priest will let me ride with him again if I tell him I want to.

"How far from the city are we?" I ask instead.

"Half an hour."

"Hmm," I hum, closing my eyes to soak in the morning sun. "I wonder if they'll still let me register for classes without my admission letter and ID. The cop from yesterday probably never even filed the report about the kids who robbed me."

Priest is silent for a long time, and I force my eyes open to look at him. I am shocked to find his eyes hard and jaw clenched, as if he's moments away from a fight, but that's not what has me sitting up straight.

No, it's the way my body reacts to this look on him.

His eyes are dark and cold, they have no business sending a tremble down to my knees or the wet heat pooling in my core.

Christ, since when do I like big scary men?

"What did you say?" he growls dangerously, and my nipples pucker. I gasp, mortified at my body's reaction to his rough voice.

"W-what?"

My eyes drop to his clenched fists, and I swallow deeply at the memory of those same calloused hands strumming my body with such expertise . . . I want them on me again.

I'd called him Daddy as he buried that firm mouth between my thighs and took me to a whole different universe. Would he want to do that again? Christ, I am trembling just thinking about it.

Snap out of it, Sky!

"You just said you got robbed. I want you to tell me what happened."

Wetness spreads between my legs, staining my inner thighs, and I fiddle with the hem of my borrowed

T-shirt—the second one I've had to take from Priest since he destroyed the first last night—and fight the onslaught of senses on my body. I force my thighs together and stare wide-eyed at Priest, trying to make sense of what he's telling me.

He wants . . . something.

"Uh . . . I . . ." My mind goes blank. I have no idea what we're talking about.

I can see his mouth moving, heck, I can even hear the words, but my lust-addled brain can't think past his deep rumbly voice and the effects it has on me.

Focus!

Christ, I want to. I'm trying, but ever since Priest touched me, he seems to have aroused something in me, and all I can think about is his hands on me. Especially when he watches me the way he is.

"Sky, are you okay?" Priest asks, closing the distance between us and placing his massive palm over my forehead, and a tremble rocks my body from the simple touch.

"I'm fine," I whisper shakily, placing the ice cream on a small table just so I have something to do with my hands.

"You're shaking," he says roughly, and I have to admit it's quite a sight to witness this man worry over me. No one's done that for me since Nana died. "You need to drink something warm and perhaps get more rest. After the night you had—"

"No, I'm fine," I say, or at least, I will be when he drops the hand he's trailing down my neck.

"You're clearly not."

"I am. I'm just . . ." Heat rises in my neck and cheeks, and I can practically feel them turning a deeper shade of pink.

His eyes light up with realization, and the worry clears from his hard face, lust settling in its place. My lips part in a gasp when Priest reaches for me and hauls me onto his lap, a tremble rushing down my spine when my sex rubs against his erection. Between us, I am the one who is practically naked, dressed only in his shirt, and even though we're technically outside with any number of men nearby, I find that I don't care to hide my need as I rock against him.

"Princess," he says gruffly, sliding his fingers into my hair, grabbing a fistful and tugging gently, forcing my head to fall back. I whimper when he leans in and kisses a path down my neck. "If all you wanted was Daddy's touch, all you had to do was ask."

His free hand cups my backside, and I whimper as he massages my ass, sending pleasure rocking up my body.

"Please, Daddy," I moan when he drags his tongue over the smooth column of my throat.

"Want me to fuck you right here, where anyone could walk by and see you riding my cock?" I bite into my lip to fight back a moan when his mouth closes around my earlobe and he nips at the skin, soothing it with his tongue. "I bet they would love a show, watching their president wreck your tight little pussy as I suck those perfect nipples into my mouth."

"Oh, God!" His words will wreck me before the rest of him can.

"I want to hear the sounds you'll make when I drive my cock into you," he says hoarsely against my skin, which sends my body trembling with need. "Everyone in camp will hear your—"

I whine when his words cut off, and I have no idea why he would stop until someone clears their throat.

My face burns with mortification, and I bury my head in Priest's shoulder so I don't have to face whoever it is that walked up on me grinding against Priest's erection like a cat in heat.

"Prez, we have a . . . situation," calls out a voice, but I don't dare look up or turn around to see who it is.

Priest lets out a frustrated groan, and I can feel his body practically vibrate with frustration, but his sense of duty takes precedence. "What is it, Knight?"

"It's about the packages we brought in last night." I notice the man hesitate to speak for a moment, what with me being right here, but Priest's hand is still firm on my ass, making it hard for me to get up and run away. Knight must figure I'm not going anywhere because he carries on. "If we don't take care of them right away, we'll have the Black Chains knocking down our doors. One of them is the nephew of their president."

"Fuck!" Priest curses before nodding at the man. "Go on ahead, I'll be there in five."

I hear the man walk away, and I expect Priest to put me down and follow, but instead, the man climbs to his feet with me clinging to him and carries me into the house. I wrap my legs around his hips as he carries me into the living room, gasping when my back suddenly hits the wall.

"It's okay, you can go ahead, and I'll—Oh!"

"I have five minutes to take care of you, princess," Priest growls, taking my lips in a hard wet kiss, and I am too weak to resist him. I offer my mouth needily, meeting the hungry stroke of his tongue with fevered moans. "I can't leave you wanting, can I?"

"Oh, Daddy," I whimper in between kisses, pleasure rocking my body when he tears away the shirt. At this rate, he'll have no shirts left, but I am not complaining. Something about this man going all caveman does something to me. I imagine it does the same thing to him too as I can feel his cock thickening against my thigh.

He guides me to take the shirt off where it drapes around my shoulders, leaving me completely naked, but I can't focus on that as his hands are already busy.

I cry out when he palms my breast, rubbing circles over my aching nipples, and when he drops his head, taking the left bud into his warm mouth, I nearly lose it.

"Hmm," he groans around the aching peak, his throaty voice sending a rush of heat to my sex, driving me closer and closer to a point of insanity.

"More, Daddy," I beg.

Christ, how are we going to do this in five minutes? How am I going to convince myself that I've had enough when five minutes are done? I doubt that a lifetime would be enough to spend with this man.

"I'll show you more, princess," Priest breathes, kissing a trail down my body, and when he lifts my body up so my legs are thrown over his shoulders, I nearly scream. My eyes widen at the position, and I know he is built like a god with chiseled muscles over his entire body, but . . . there is no way he is about to do *that* in this position—

A scream rips from my throat when I feel his tongue lick a trail along my sex. It's wet and hot and . . . Oh, God! It's somehow ten times more intense than last night.

There are no gentle kisses to ease me into it.

Priest is like a man possessed as he buries his face between my legs, licking and sucking at my sex like a starved animal. He finds new ways to drive me to the brink with his tongue as he stiffens it before flicking my trembling clit so hard, I have to slap a hand on my mouth to stop the scream that builds up in my throat.

"Daddy," I sob, my heels digging into his back as he teases the bundle of nerves I had no idea were so sensitive until I met this man. "Yes, Daddy!"

My back arches off the wall as he devours me, lapping at my arousal with the flat of his tongue, and when his mouth closes around my clit and sucks, that's all it takes to send me careening over the edge as the world explodes around me.

This man wrecks me. His tongue strokes me through the orgasm and leaves me a quivering mess. Priest slowly lowers me to my feet, and it's a wonder I don't plummet to the floor what with the way my knees are trembling.

"Goddamn, princess, you're so perfect when you come apart in my arms." He brushes his lips over mine, and I can taste myself on his tongue when he deepens the kiss. "When I come back, you better be ready for me. I'll not stop until I have shot my seed inside your tight little cunt and marked you as mine."

With a last peck to the lips, Priest turns around and leaves me panting against the wall. I barely make it upstairs to his bedroom and close the door before my knees give in and I slowly slide down the wall.

It should terrify me.

This world I have stumbled into should scare the hell out of me and send me running back to my small town, and yet, all I can think about is when I'll see Priest again.

The gentle giant that has so quickly wormed his way into my heart.

Chapter Six

Priest

"I'm in a terrible mood, so you better start talking," I say, walking into the Barn, eyes on the three men kneeling on the cold hard floor before me.

The Barn, as we call our interrogation building, is a small structure situated in a remote corner of the MC's private property. These days, with the club edging more and more toward legitimate business, we rarely need to use the Barn for its intended purpose. But the need still arises more often than I'd like.

The Barn is a small structure, roughly twenty feet square. There's a concrete floor with a drain in the center and soundproofed, tin walls. The room is devoid of any natural light, and whatever unfortunate soul is inside won't be able to tell what time of the day it is. It's basically a metal box, and it's hot as fuck. Only the club's senior officials have access to the Barn or even know of its existence.

It's been a while since I have been called to visit the Barn; I'm usually content to leave its occupants for the club's enforcers to deal with. Today, I'm not in the best mood. My fingers are itching for a fight, and the men kneeling on the floor must sense it too because they try to shuffle back when their eyes lock on me, but there is nowhere to go. They are trapped.

"W-we don't know anything," the oldest of the three men blurts. He can't be a year over thirty, but his sunburned face and thinning hair make him look haggard.

"We both know that's not true," I say, rolling my sleeves up. "But perhaps you need my help to remember."

There is no remorse as I work over the men. There is little moral code when it comes to criminals, but kidnapping innocent people and trafficking them is not something the Steel Order MC will abide. Most clubs in our area don't, but the Black Chains will do anything for money.

By the time I am done, I have a list of names of all the people who aided the men in trafficking the girls last night and the date for the next transfer.

"What do we do about the nephew?" Knight asks stepping up to me and nodding at a whimpering young man on the floor. "We don't want to bring a fight to our doorstep because of some dumb kid."

"Get rid of the other two, then send this one back to his uncle with the message to stay out of our territory," I tell him. "The Black Chains need to know what happens when you cross us."

Knight nods and calls Reaper to help deal with the mess.

Normally, this would be the end of it. As our rivals, the Black Chains expect us to retaliate if caught on our turf, so sending their president's nephew back to him broken and bloody—but alive—would be seen simply as the Steel Order defending our territory. We don't make it a habit to get involved in social justice matters considering the illegal businesses we dabble in ourselves, but I won't stand by and watch as innocent young girls are kidnapped and sold.

And Sky . . . she's one of us.

She's mine!

And I need her now. Beating these idiots has done nothing to settle the raging storm in my head, and I know just where I need to go to calm down, but before I can leave, someone steps in my path.

Knight's serious expression draws me up short, and I can see there is something on his mind. "What?" I ask with a sigh.

"Look man, you know I don't normally worry about your hookups, but that girl . . ."

"What about her?"

"I ran a background check on her," he says, bracing himself for a verbal lashing, but I stay calm, waiting for him to finish what he needs to say. "We've been best friends for twenty years, and I know that, while you're not completely an asshole, you don't really give a shit about many people, so when you brought the girl back with you, I was curious about her. I called our connection at the police department to look into her."

My face remains blank to hide just how much I hate that my best friend went behind my back to run a background check on my girl, but a logical part of me reminds me that I would have done the same thing. We never let anyone who is not family into the clubhouse, all casual hookups happen off the property with discretion.

Bringing a total stranger into our space was reckless, but I don't regret it. I would do the same thing over again.

Sky is mine!

"So, what did you find out?" I ask, impatient to get back to the girl in my house.

"Sky Tyler is her name, in case your hands and mouth were too busy to ask." He snickers. "Anyway, she's just your typical girl from a small town who found bad luck in the big city. She made a police report yesterday about getting robbed."

"What does the report say?"

Knight's expression lifts with his humor. "Apparently, she arrived in the city, and within hours, decided to trust a bunch of teens to carry her stuff, and they disappeared into the crowd with all her things."

I shake my head at her naivety, but she doesn't have to worry about people taking advantage of her anymore. Not when she has the scariest motherfucker in the city eating out of her palms.

"Do we know the cop that handed her over to the Black Chains?"

"Not yet," Knight says, dipping his hands into his pockets as a dark scowl overtakes his features. "You'll have to ask her what he looked like. According to our guy, everyone who was on shift last night was accounted for the entire time, and the spot for the name of the officer taking the report was left blank. I'm having our boys see if they can track down the kids who took off with her bags."

I nod, glad he's already taking care of it. I slap his shoulder and start for the clubhouse, my mind already on the girl in my suite.

It seems Sky hasn't had the best welcome to Austin, and I am about to fix that for her. By the time I am done, she'll forget all about the bad things that have happened to her.

***

I find her curled up in my bed.

I stop by the door to stare at her, and my heart thumps in my chest at the beauty lying in my space. She is magnificent, her long golden hair cascading over the pillow and a soft smile playing on her lips.

I should walk away.

What I should do and what I want to do are sentiments constantly at war when it comes to this girl.

Walking away is not an option. Not at this moment, not ever.

I quietly approach her, gently brushing a strand of hair away from her face. She stirs slightly but doesn't wake up. I lean down and brush my lips over hers before trailing them down her neck and soaking up her intoxicating scent. She moans in her sleep, the voice light and needy.

"Daddy," she whimpers, and fuck, hearing her call out to me even in her sleep shoots straight to my cock, but it's the aching clench of my heart that comes as a surprise. I've never truly been needed by anyone.

Sure, the club needs me as their president, the members depend on me for leadership, but if something ever happened to me, I could easily be replaced, just like I replaced my old man when he was arrested and sentenced to life. My younger sister, Rhea, briefly needed me when she was forced to flee her mother and stepfather. But she's always been pretty independent, she even goes to college out of state.

For Sky to seek me out even in her sleep tugs at my heartstrings, and I fall deeper for the girl.

"Mine," I whisper possessively as I run my hands over her covered thighs, even as I brush my lips over her throat, slowly waking her up.

"Priest," she moans, and when I push up to look at her, my eyes lock on clear light blue ones, and I find myself sinking into them. Christ, everything about this girl is perfect. Pure. As if to make up for the imperfections I bring to the table.

"You're up," I say throatily, brushing my lips against hers, and she opens up to me so easily, sighing with pleasure when I slip my hand under the sheets, my cock jutting hard against my jeans when I find her naked under the covers.

She parts her thighs for me when I slide my hands down her body, gasping softly against my lips when I rub circles over her damp folds to part her feminine lips. She whimpers when I begin rubbing circles over her sex, coating my hand with her arousal.

"Oh, Daddy," she cries, arching her hips to ride my fingers, and it takes everything not to shoot in my pants.

My cock is straining painfully behind my fly with the need to come inside of her tight little cunt and mark her as mine.

"Fuck!" I growl, withdrawing my hand before tossing the covers off her to reveal her naked body. "I need to fuck you now, baby." My eyes stay on her as I push back off the bed to strip out of my clothes. I tear off the shirt and toss it aside. "Touch yourself, princess. Get your tight pussy ready for Daddy."

She bites her lips and looks down, but not before I catch sight of her excited eyes. She hesitates a little, and I watch with bated breath as my perfect girl dips her left hand between her legs.

"Do it just how I showed you," I say gruffly, unzipping my jeans as I watch her try to mimic my moves from earlier, and soon, she's not just doing it for show. Her back arches and her nipples bead as she drags her middle finger through her folds.

"Oh," she cries, her eyes glazing over as her breath quickens.

I take out my cock and stroke it as I approach her, my control torn to shreds. I have been hard off and on all day, her body teasing me even as I fought for patience.

"You drive me crazy, little girl," I rasp, climbing onto bed and settling one knee between her thighs. I push her legs further apart, forcing her to withdraw her hand from her body which she does with a low whine. "Only I am allowed to bring you pleasure."

My mouth is pressed down on hers before she can protest or say a word. She wraps her arms around my shoulders as I align my throbbing cock with her sex, rubbing the thick head over her arousal to gather her wetness. Lord above, just being so close to the prize drives me wild.

I've never, in all of my thirty-five years of living, needed one single person the way I need this girl. In less than twenty-four hours, she went from being someone I didn't know existed to being my entire world.

A girl I would kill for. No, that would be too simple. Sky is someone I would die for.

"Oh!" she whimpers when I push the head of my shaft against her tight entrance, and I begin to press into her. Barely. I can tell this is not going to be easy for either one of us with how freaking tight she is.

"Fuck, princess, you're so tight!" I grind out, bracing an arm over her head and fight not to thrust the rest of the way in and bury my cock in her warmth. My desires aside, the thought of hurting Sky in any way that doesn't bring her pleasure sends my stomach churning.

"It's okay, Daddy," she whispers breathily, and Christ, she looks like the most beautiful thing in the world, naked beneath me, the entrance of her tight little cunt stretched by my cock. "I know it's supposed to hurt. I'm okay."

I lean down and brush my lips against hers, our breaths mingling hotly as I wrap my free arm around her thigh and slide another inch into her tightness. "I'll make you feel better soon, sweetheart," I rasp shakily, pushing more of my length into her slickness.

"So big!" she gasps, her fingers flexing around my shoulders.

I bury my face in her neck just as I thrust my hips forward and rip through the thin barrier of her innocence. She cries out, burying her nails in my shoulders as my balls threaten to empty from the feel of her squeezing my hard shaft. She's so fucking slick and tight it's a miracle that I haven't already come.

"Oh . . . Oh God!" she cries, dragging her short nails down my back as I hold still to give her time to adjust to my thickness.

"Are you okay, princess?"

"Yeah," she hums, rocking her hips slightly, and the move has my balls throbbing with the need to come.

"Going to fuck you now, princess," is all the warning she gets before my fingers tighten around her thigh and I start rocking into her sex, gently at first until I can't stand it anymore. Something feral, almost inhuman rises in me, and soon, I am hammering into her tight little cunt in fast fevered moves.

I've waited for—wanted—this perfect angel from the second she wrapped her arms around my shoulders and hugged me like the sun revolves around me.

Like she was the lucky one to meet me and not the other way around.

"Daddy . . . feels good," she sobs, her hips lifting to meet mine, and just like that, we forget everything else but this moment. I pump recklessly into her tight channel, her pleasured cries guiding me around her body.

"Going to breed you, princess." I growl. "Bury my seed so deep inside of you and get you all swollen with my child."

"Yes. *yes!*" she chants, tearing her nails down my back and no doubt adding to the battle scars that already mar my skin, but she can mark me all she wants. Hers are the only scars I will proudly carry.

I'm so close.

Fuck! I knew I wouldn't last long with how tight and responsive to my touch she is.

I lower my head to kiss her neck, trailing my lips down the slope of her collarbone. She cries out when my mouth closes hotly over her nipple, sucking at the tight bud until she's mewling and thrashing under me. I give the same attention to the other nipple as I pick up my pace, driving my cock into her harder and faster.

I release her nipple with a slick pop before lifting my eyes to lock with hers. "I need you to come for Daddy," I rasp, tightening my hand on her hip as I rock harder into her, rutting her like a madman and sending the bed creaking under us. Her breathing grows labored and her thighs start shaking before she climaxes with a sob, her pussy cinching hard around my cock and triggering my own orgasm.

I come with a roar, my body straining hard as I spill the thick ropes of my hot seed into her trembling pussy. I pump my cock roughly into her tightness, her sobs mingling with my groans as I draw out the orgasm. A shudder racks my body as she milks me of every drop, and it seems to last forever.

"Mine!" I grind harshly, pressing my lips hard against hers and swallowing her pleasured cries. "You belong to only me, Sky. I will bury anyone that fucking dares to touch you."

"Yours," she whimpers, wrapping her arms tightly around me as I drop on top of her in exhaustion.

I brush my lips over her temples, vowing to protect this girl to my last breath. I was a dangerous man before, but now that I have so much to lose, I am practically lethal. I have never wanted to protect anything or anyone as much as I want to protect Sky, and anyone who gets in the way of that will be signing their own death warrant.

Mine!

Chapter Seven

Sky

"So, blondie, how did you get robbed by a bunch of kids?"

I study the tall dark haired man and question how he and Priest came to be best friends. The two couldn't be any more opposite if they tried. Their similarities end at their massive builds and their love for bikes.

Where Priest is built like a tank with more of a buzz cut, his best friend and VP, Knight, is more on the leaner side with long dark hair and a charming smile that no doubt has all the girls running to him.

But there is something unsettling about the man. While his smiling might be disarming, if you look long enough, you can catch a peak behind the facade. His eyes say that Knight is the kind of man who will stab you with a wide smile on his face and love every second he spends watching you bleed to death in front of him. The thought sends a shudder through my body, and I lean closer to Priest, forcing my gaze away from his clearly unhinged best friend.

"The kids seemed nice, and they were so polite when I approached them," I murmur, sliding my hand around Priest's as I stare into the bonfire.

Ever since we had sex, I've been feeling especially clingy to the man.

A part of me expected Priest to grow tired of me and disappear under the guise of "club business," but he's been by my side all afternoon, and when he brought me outside for the bonfire with people he considers his family, I dared imagine that something has shifted between us.

I want to ask him, but I don't know where to start.

Liking someone . . . feeling a sense of belonging . . .

It's all new to me.

I shake my head as though to be rid of the thoughts and focus on the moment. Sitting by the bonfire, I can feel the warmth on my skin from both the crackling flames dancing in front of me and the massive man whose skin is like a furnace.

The scent of burning wood fills the air, mingling with the faint aroma of grilled food. Around us, I see a large gathering of bikers, their leather vests adorned with club patches, laughing and sharing stories. Women and children wander about, which shocked me at first, but Priest explained that gatherings like this are a regular occurrence and a way for the MC to bond. I think the fact that so many children are comfortable running and playing, weaving in and out of groups of rough and ready bikers says a lot about who these men are.

Everyone has been so welcoming to me. All of the women present are married to or dating someone in the club. I had expected them to be a little wary, maybe even a bit territorial, but that hasn't been the case. In fact, one of the women even told me she was thrilled to finally see Priest with someone. I hadn't known how to respond to that, so I'd just smiled and hurried to find Priest.

"Didn't your family teach you not to trust anyone when you arrive in the city?" Knight asks, clearly not done tormenting me.

"Please let it go," I groan, dropping my head on Priest's shoulder even as I throw a glare his best friend's way.

"I'm just saying, everyone knows you don't take your eyes off your things for even a second in Austin."

"I've learned my lesson, Knight," I whine, pleading with him to let it go, but he opens his mouth like he's going to say something else. It's not until Priest glares in his direction that he finally drops it. "Are there always so many people at these cookouts?" I ask, fascinated by this community I stumbled into.

"We do this every week, but it's usually a smaller group. Not everyone can make it every time. However, *someone* had the genius idea to call a full-family gathering just to introduce his girl to the club."

My heart skips a couple of beats at Knight's words, and I stare straight at the fire, my cheeks flaming, and it has little to do with the heat from the bonfire.

This cookout . . . is for me?

The thought of Priest doing this to introduce me to his brothers has me biting my lower lip to hide the grin that threatens to break free, and the fact that he doesn't try to negate Knight's claim only makes me believe the words must be true.

I've hardly spoken to any of the other bikers, what with me bickering with Knight all evening, and I've been glued by Priest's side, leaving no doubt what I am to the man.

His.

He called me his this afternoon, and now, everyone else knows that too.

Priest is like no man I have met in my life. He doesn't make empty promises, but instead, leaves his actions to speak for themselves. Every little thing he's done leaves me floored, and I want to show him just how much all this means to me.

How much *he* means to me.

I can't do anything here, though. Not with so many people surrounding us, so I push down my nerves and turn to Priest to find his dark eyes already fixed on me. That is all it takes for a wave of warmth to wash over my body, leaving me confused about how one man can draw such a reaction from me.

He hasn't even touched me yet, and my body is already trembling.

"Can you show me around?" I ask him, my voice huskier than I've ever heard it, and Priest must catch the need in my tone because his thick brows go up.

"Sure, let's go," he says, getting up from the log we're seated on and helping me up as well.

"Can I come too?" Knight calls out with a laugh, and I flash him a mock glare while Priest simply ignores him.

My heart is beating in my throat as Priest leads me away from the crowd and the loud music, but I find the nerves die down, and in its place, desire settles. Anticipation of what's going to happen once we're out of view has my body practically shaking with need. How I went from never kissing anyone my entire life to wanting to climb this mountain of a man at every opportunity confuses me.

It grows eerily silent the further we get from the crowd. "The bonfire was nice," I say in an attempt to fill the silence. "Everyone was so nice to me, well, except for Knight."

Priest doesn't respond, and his silence has my brows drawing in confusion. Now that I think about it, he really hasn't said much tonight, and I'm starting to think I might have said something wrong.

"Priest—" I start, but my words are cut off when I am grabbed by the shoulders and pushed gently against a brick wall. A rush of air escapes my lips at the contact, and my eyes are wide when they lock with his darker ones in the dim light.

"Tonight was about staking a claim," he says gruffly, sending a warm tingle racing up my body. "In our world, a biker does not introduce his woman to his brothers unless he intends for it to be permanent."

I suck in a sharp breath at his words.

"P-permanent?"

"All your problems, insecurities, and fears belong to me now, and by extension, to everyone in the Steel Order MC. We're your family now, princess."

Permanent. Family.

My eyes fill up as I try to wrap my head around his words. Nothing in life is permanent, but especially not in my life. My parents died when I was a little girl, and then Nana, leaving me to take care of myself. A job I have been terrible at, and what Priest is telling me . . .

I'm terrified to believe him. To believe that I could finally have a home—a family—I don't have to worry about losing.

"A family," I whisper, sliding my arms around his neck and offering my lips to the man who I think stole my heart the first moment our eyes met. Priest wraps his arms around my waist and pulls me closer, taking my lips in a hungry kiss that sends my toes curling with pleasure. His hand digs into my waist as he deepens the kiss, our tongues meeting in a slick slide that makes me whimper with need.

"You're mine, princess," he rasps between kisses. His left hand goes up to cup my tits through my shirt, and I have to quickly break the hold I have on him to grab his hand before he can tear another shirt. I'd only just gotten some clothes I could wear this afternoon, a loan from one of the other biker's wives. "Fuck, you're killing me, little girl."

I bite his lower lip, liking the way he says that a little too much. "I'm not letting you destroy another shirt like some animal," I whisper, brushing my lips over his jaw and cheek.

"I can buy you more," he says roughly, pushing his erection against my inner thigh, and I can feel him grow harder and thicker by the second. "I need you naked now."

I look around, and although we're in a pretty dark spot tucked around the side of the house, I can still see the bonfire in the distance. "Priest . . ."

"Strip, or I will tear it off myself."

My fingers scramble to pull the fabric over my head so my top half is naked, and since I am not wearing a bra, I shudder at the cold air that touches my nipples. I feel the need to hide them even if it's just us two, but the feeling disappears the second his hands are on me, and just like that . . . nothing else matters.

Nothing but the fingers circling my nipples. "Oh, God!" I cry out, my knees growing weak when he tugs my left nipple between his knuckles. When he drops his mouth to my breast, my knees do buckle, and he has to grab me before I can slide down to the ground. I slap a hand on my mouth to conceal my cries when Priest starts licking at my aching bud, rolling his tongue around the peak and driving me as close to insanity as I can get. "Want you, Daddy!"

Pleasure rushes down my core before sending a needy shudder up my spine when he starts kissing a path down my body. "You're so fucking gorgeous, princess," he whispers harshly against my skin before dropping to his knees on the hard ground. "And now you're mine."

He kisses my stomach as he starts unzipping my jeans and tugging them down. I step out of them, leaving me naked and completely exposed to a man who's fully dressed, but when he lifts my left leg to his shoulder and starts kissing my inner thigh, I forget that little fact.

He has that way about him. A single brush of skin is enough to fry all my brain cells, and nothing beyond his touch makes sense.

Christ, he doesn't even have to touch me for that to happen. All I have to do is look at him.

Priest is built like a Greek god, with broad shoulders and thick arms whose strength I have witnessed firsthand. He towers over me, and I had no idea just how much I was into that until the first time I had to get on my tippy toes to kiss him.

Mine!

Only I get to see this dangerous biker this way. Only I get to feel the brush of his lips against my inner thighs, making their way up to my wet and trembling sex.

"*Yes*, Daddy!" I cry out, my back arching when I feel the long glide of his tongue over the valley of my sex. There is little I can do to bite back the moan that rises in my throat when he starts licking my sex like a possessed man, my pussy growing slick with arousal when he starts rubbing at my clit with the pad of his thumb.

Oh!

Oh, God, this is too much! It's even more intense from the adrenaline of the thought of someone from the party catching us.

I bet he wouldn't stop. Something tells me that Priest wouldn't be mortified at someone finding him on his knees, me desperate for him as he laps at my sex like it's the one thing he needs to live, driving my body closer and closer to the edge.

I grip his head with both hands and start rocking my hips when the pressure starts building to a peak, and the final straw is when he slides his middle finger into my sex. My walls cinch hard around his finger even as my eyes roll back from the explosion that rocks my body.

I scream as he jacks his thick digit in and out of my channel in fast, rough moves as his tongue teases the trembling bud of nerves. My toes curl, and I feel it to the tips of my hair.

I have no idea how long my body trembles as I seem to lose sense of time, and the next thing I know, he's filling me with every last inch of his thick erection. His dark eyes bore into mine as he starts driving his cock fast and hard into me, and I don't believe I can feel more, but it seems Priest is set on taking on the challenge.

What is happening to me?

My body is still shaking from the first earth-shuttering climax, and Priest is determined to bring me back to the edge, promising to send me plummeting from an even higher precipice.

"Goddamn, princess, you rode Daddy's tongue so well," he whispers crudely, pinning me to the side of the house and driving his cock into my sex in fast hungry thrusts that send pleasure shooting up my body. "Going to fuck you so hard, you'll be feeling me all week!"

I wrap my arms around his shoulders to brace myself as he rocks hard into me, letting out a low whine when he suddenly stops. "Daddy. . .!"

"Shh," he pants, cupping my mouth with his palm, and it takes me a second to realize why we've stopped. There is a group of bikers walking in our direction.

I gasp behind his palm as the men approach us, and although we're well hidden in the shadows, I am not exactly confident we are fully out of sight.

I can feel Priest's length pulse inside of me, and when he starts moving again, slowly this time, my eyes snap wide open. He inches his rigid shaft out of me before sinking back in slowly and torturously, making my eyes roll back.

There is no way he's going to keep going with the men walking so close to our spot, right?

"Be quiet for Daddy, okay?" he purrs into my ear as he rolls his hips, and I barely suppress a moan from the pleasure that shoots up my core. I throw my head back as he drags his tongue down my throat, all the while thrusting into me in slow measured moves. "Don't make a sound, or they'll stop to check."

I whimper at his words, the thought of getting caught exciting me in ways it shouldn't.

"My dirty little girl, you like that."

I shake my head, but the truth is in how fast my pulse thrums and the way I move my hips to meet his thrust.

Priest removes his palm and replaces it with his mouth, kissing me hard and making me forget that we're trying to hide. I moan into the kiss as he starts pumping faster and harder into my sex, driving his thickness into me until I feel myself teeter close to the edge once more.

He breaks the kiss and drops his head to my shoulder as he slaps into me hard, chanting whispered promises against my neck, his hot breath on my skin stroking the blazing fire until it bursts free.

"Daddy! *Oh, God!*"

I clap a hand on my mouth as my body shudders with another orgasm a second before his muscles seize and we're both falling. He sinks his teeth into my neck, masking the roar I feel rattle in his chest. His body flexes against mine, and I marvel at how beautiful he is when he falls apart along with me.

"Fuck, baby," he heaves into my neck, rocking his shaft into me and filling me with his seed. "Going to get you pregnant. Breed you and keep you with me forever."

Our bodies spasm together, and it takes forever for us to calm down. It's not until I've stopped shaking that I remember the men who walked by.

"Oh my God, Priest, do you think they heard us?" I whisper, mortified by the thought.

"No, they did not," Priest assures me, brushing his lips against mine, showing me a much softer side that I bet most people will never see from my rough biker. "You're mine, princess. I'll protect you with my life."

I believe him.

And when he says he wants to take me back to his house and recreate the scene all over again, I believe that too.

Chapter Eight

Priest

What has this girl done to me?

In a span of a few days, I've gone from taking on rival MCs like the Black Chains to now terrorizing baby-faced teens, who seem like they're one threat away from peeing their pants.

"That's all we took, sir," the taller of the two kids sniffs, tears streaming down his face as he points at the three bags lying on the floor. "Everything is in there. Please don't kill us!"

I shake my head at the scene playing out in front of me and turn to face Knight, who is responsible for bringing the kids here. The idea was to get Sky's stolen items back and let the petty thieves off with just a warning. They are harmless kids who get a thrill from stealing from tourists, and we're not in the business of dealing with petty thieves.

"Why did you bring them here?" I ask, exasperated by my best friend.

"Well, someone had to carry all the shit your girlfriend lost, and it wasn't going to be me."

"Your girlfriend!" one of the kids yells, his eyes widening with fear. "We're so sorry, sir. We had no idea she was your girlfriend."

I shake my head and rub two fingers on my temples with a tired sigh. It's only seven in the morning, and I'm already tired. With another sigh, I look around and spot two prospects at a distance, calling them over to give the kids a ride back to the city.

I wait until they're gone before turning to Knight. We've been friends long enough that I'm pretty much used to his antics, but he's my VP because he always gets the job done. Sometimes I think there is something wrong with him, and perhaps I should be more worried about that, but then again, he is custom-made for the job.

Who else would have caught a couple of petty thieves in a city of almost a million people?

"Thanks, man," I say when I know he's expecting me to point out that he brought strangers into our clubhouse. I can overlook that considering the fact that he did this as a favor to me. I could have easily asked a prospect to look into this for me, but I know it would have taken forever to get all of Sky's items back, if we ever managed it at all.

"Sky's family now," he says with a shrug before adding, "And now you owe me." He waves as he turns around to leave, and I have no doubt he will cash in on the favor at the most inconvenient time.

Knowing my best friend, he'll most definitely ask for something crazy.

With a shake of my head, I grab all of Sky's items and make the trip back to my house. After the cookout, it didn't feel right making Sky stay with me in my suite at the clubhouse, and I decided it was time to move back into the house I'd bought when my little sister came to live with me, the one I'd abandoned when she'd left for college. Sky and I moved in the next day.

The scent of coffee and bacon hits me when I walk through the door ten minutes later. I drop everything in the living room and follow the smell to the kitchen, where I find the girl that's wormed her way into my heart standing at the stove, dressed in yet another one of my shirts.

A strange possessive feeling takes over, and I am tempted to hide all her bags so she never wears any of her clothes ever again. Fuck, she looks so cozy in my clothes, her hair slightly tousled from sleep.

I could stand here all day and watch her, I realize.

Sky is a sight to behold. The morning sunlight streaming through the window casts a warm glow over her, and my heart catches in my throat as I watch her move gracefully around the kitchen. When she spots me, a radiant smile graces her lips, sucking all the air from my lungs.

"You're back," she says, the smile spreading across her face when I start for her. The air fills with the sound of her laughter when I wrap my arms around her from behind. All the blood rushing south when she wiggles her ass against my cock.

"What are you doing?" I rasp, rocking my hardening cock against her pert ass.

"I'm making us breakfast. Nana always said the way to a man's heart is through his stomach," she says, swatting my hand when it starts a slow descent from her stomach. "And no, there will be no playing around until after breakfast."

I spin her around so she's facing me. "You've already wormed your way into my heart, Sky. You don't need food to achieve that."

Her eyes flash with surprise, but I don't let her think too much of it as I lean down and take that perfect mouth with mine. Despite her earlier warning, she whimpers into the kiss, opening for me as I drag our tongues together in a move so erotic, it's darn near sinful.

Fuck, I will never get enough of these perfect lips. Five, ten, or even twenty years from today, I will still crave the feel of her soft lips against my firm ones. The little breathy noises she makes when I stroke our tongues together will always send my cock throbbing with need.

I cup her cheek as I deepen the kiss, savoring her taste and just how perfectly she responds to me.

"Priest . . . breakfast," she breathes between kisses, gasping when I grab her hips and lift her to the kitchen counter.

"Breakfast can wait," I growl, running my large, calloused hands up the soft skin of her thighs to her sex. Her thighs part for me, and she moans against my lips when I rub my middle finger over her wetness. "Need to be inside of you. Right now."

"Ah!" she cries when I slip my finger into her tight sex, holding her still with my other hand.

It's like I can't get enough of this girl.

Before Sky, I was involved with other women, but it was all casual, and my hookups were few and far between. I never found myself craving the company of one woman, and we both knew what we were getting from each other was for the moment, but with Sky . . .

I can't help but think of the future.

Every time I kiss her, I crave more. Her pleasure is more important than mine. No, her pleasure *is* mine.

Watching her arch her back, her throat exposed and nipples pushing hard against my shirt as she rides my thick digit is the hottest thing I have ever seen. I could spend a lifetime—and I plan to—finding different ways to pleasure her body. To witness her big sky blue eyes roll back with desire . . . for me.

"Fuck me, Daddy, please," she sobs, her thighs trembling with the need to come. I withdraw my finger from her body, making quick work of my zipper, almost tearing off the darn thing as I tug it down.

"You're so fucking gorgeous, princess," I rasp heavily, guiding my thick length to her opening. I wrap an arm around her waist before driving my hips forward and impaling her with my fat cock. My eyes roll back from the tight heat surrounding my swollen shaft. Her pussy pulses needily around me, and the grip of her snug sex almost sends my heavy balls exploding.

She wraps her legs around my hips when I start to rock into her wetness, the sound of our love making both obscene and sinful, but it only fuels me.

"Faster, Daddy," she cries, wrapping an arm around my shoulder and leaning up to meet my thrusts. Her face is twisted in pleasure as I pinch her nipples through the shirt, tugging the tight bud between my knuckles and causing her to cry out in pleasure.

Our eyes lock as I drive into her, faster and harder, pushing us closer and closer to the edge until she's climaxing with a sob, her sex cinching hard around my throbbing cock. My gut twists in a pain-pleasure that burns through me as I come with a roar, spilling hot ropes of my seed into her womb. Our bodies ripple from the power of our orgasms, and I realize I never want to share this feeling with anyone but her.

My head drops to her shoulder as she drops her legs from my hips. "I love you, Sky," I breathe into her neck. "You're everything to me."

A long beat of silence passes before she finally speaks. "Y-you love me?"

"I told you we became a family last night. Why is it so unbelievable that I would be in love with you?"

"No, it's just . . ." she sobs out a laugh that rocks her entire body. "I love you too, Priest."

"Good, because I have something to show you," I say, pushing back from the counter. I take her hand,

and we walk to the bathroom to quickly clean up, and when we make our way back to the kitchen, she does not notice the large bags in the living room until I've pointed them out.

She stands still for a few seconds before turning to me, stunned. "H-how?"

"The kids said they didn't take anything, so check and let me know if anything is missing."

"How did you . . . I didn't . . . Oh my God!"

Her eyes fill up with tears as she turns to look at me, and all I can think is there is nothing I wouldn't do for her. There is so much love and adoration in her eyes that it floors me.

"Knight got hold of the kids and made them return your things."

She smiles tearfully at me before wrapping her arms around me in a tight hug. "I guess I can forgive him for all that teasing at the bonfire," she whispers, her lips brushing my neck. "Thank you."

"Of course."

She pushes back from me and walks to the bags, opening one after the other. "God, I can't believe you got everything back. I have a short window to register for classes, and they won't let me enroll after this week. I'll need to go to campus and sort out my dorm now that I have my ID back."

"I'll take you wherever it is you need to go, as long as we're on the same page that you won't be using that dorm. You live here now."

She flashes me a sweet smile before going back to checking the items in her bags. "Wow, they really didn't take anything," she muses, getting up. "I guess I can go to campus today and take care of everything."

"What will you be studying?" I ask conversationally as we walk back to the kitchen.

"Microbiology," she says excitedly. "I know it's nothing exciting, but blame it on my nana. She was a microbiologist before she moved to our little town to marry my grandfather. She had a library full of books and articles on medicine, agriculture, and environmental science. They were all I wanted to read after my parents' accident, no idea why I found them so comforting."

Her words bring me pause. "Accident?"

Sky sets to work warming up our breakfast. "The car accident that killed my parents when I was ten. Nana raised me until she died shortly after my eighteenth birthday."

"I'm sorry."

"I choose to remember the good times," she says with a soft smile. "I guess living with Nana influenced me a bit because now I want to become a microbiologist too."

I walk up to her and wrap my arms around her waist, pulling her flush against me. "You're not allowed to smile at any college boys."

"Priest!" Sky laughs, taking my statement as a joke, but I'm being serious. I'm wildly possessive, more so when it comes to her.

"I'm serious, Sky. No one is allowed to touch what's mine."

"I doubt there is one college boy that could ever live up to the president of the Steel Order. All I have to do is tell them who my boyfriend is, and they'll crash into each other trying to get away from me," she says with another laugh before turning around to brush her lips against mine. "I'm yours and yours alone."

"Good."

"Now can we have breakfast so you can finally give me that ride to campus? Knight would never let me live it down if I went on my own and got lost in Austin again."

Chapter Nine

Sky

I have dreamed of this moment all my life.

The moment I would tour the college of my dreams, walking around campus along with a bunch of other bright-eyed students as some enthusiastic kid shows us around the school grounds. The labs are everything I ever dreamed of and more.

My classes officially start next week, and the thought of finally living the dream Nana and I always talked about sends my head spinning with excitement.

A smile is splitting my face when the tour ends and the freshmen start dispersing. I told Priest he could pick me up at four, so I figure I still have an hour left to walk around and get acquainted with the space where I'm going to spend the next four years.

My first stop is the library, and it's a far cry from the public library back in Marfa. The shelves stretch endlessly, filled with books of all shapes and sizes. I lose myself in the scent of old pages and the comforting atmosphere. There are students scattered around, some reading and others with their fingers dancing across keyboards.

A light tap on the shoulder has me turning around, and I come face to face with an older lady with glasses perched on her nose. "Can I help you find anything, sweetheart?"

My lips stretch in an even bigger smile as I shake my head. "No, thank you. I'm new so I'm just looking around."

"Then look your fill, honey. I can tell you're going to be a regular."

The smile stays as I walk to the science section. I ignore the few looks I get from the male students, too excited by the library to focus on anything else.

I must lose myself because when I next check the time, I have only five minutes before Priest arrives. I give the books in the section a loving pat before rushing out of the library. It takes me longer than I'd like to admit to find the exit, but I arrive there before Priest does.

I catch the sound of the bike before I see him, and I turn to look with a smile. I spot Priest riding down the street toward me, and I entirely miss the van pulling up in front of me until I am being shoved into it.

The arms that grab me take me by surprise, and I don't have a chance to react until I am practically in the back of an SUV, kicking my feet at the man holding me.

Oh my God!

I have no idea what's happening, but fear rocks my chest like nothing I've felt before. No, that can't be true. I have been in this very situation before, and I felt this scared—helpless when the men grabbed me from the police car.

Wait . . .

Are these the same men who kidnapped me before? They can't be, can they? Perhaps they showed up to avenge their friends, and now they're going to . . . what?

Kill me?

Realizing that Priest saw the entire thing happen has my heart clenching with pain. Even when my eyes grow heavy and my breathing slower as I feel myself slowly lose consciousness, all I can think of is the man who's given me the world in such a short time.

It's okay if that's all I get in this lifetime. I won't get to have the full college experience I have craved for years, but it's fine because I got to have a taste of it, even if just for half a day.

It's okay if this is the end.

At least I got to meet the love of my life when I did.

***

I wake up to the sound of glass shattering, my eyes snapping open as I frantically look around in search of the source.

I spot a shattered bottle a few steps from where I am lying and two men pacing the floor around it, clearly anxious about something.

What happened?

Who are these men?

A skull-splitting headache has me slowly lowering my head back to the cool floor and closing my eyes in an attempt to ward it off. My brain is foggy, but I try as hard as I can to clear it. The last thing I remember is walking around the school library and the kind librarian's smile.

Priest.

My boyfriend was going to pick me up at the library entrance, but . . .

Kidnapped!

I whimper in pain as a harsh throb follows the memory, causing me to curl into myself. I can't help but question if the men hit me on the head or something, but my last memory is of one of them placing a smelly cloth over my nose and mouth.

Right, they must've drugged me. I read somewhere that it can cause headaches and nausea, but I could have done without finding out firsthand just how terrible it is.

"What the fuck do we do with her?" a voice draws me from my pity party. I figure we must be in some kind of warehouse from the way his voice echoes in the space and the concrete floor beneath me.

"I don't know! What was Prez thinking telling us to grab this girl? Do you know what he'll do to us if Priests finds out where we took his little whore?" another speaks. "The Black Chains are no match for the Steel Order. We're fucked! We should be glad no one saw us grab her."

Oh, they're dead wrong about that, but since they gave me a migraine, I'm not exactly feeling generous with information.

Even so, I have no idea why they would take me.

Revenge against Priest for taking their friends? How the hell did they even find out about me and Priest?

I have so many questions, but I don't exactly have the energy to voice them. Fortunately, I don't have to wait long to find out.

"What do you think you assholes are doing?" a new voice barks through the cavernous space. I peek my eyes open and see a short, bulky man with a long unkempt beard and thick eyebrows. He spits on the floor as he approaches the other two men, and I notice the patch on his leather vest is the same as the one the men who'd kidnapped me the first time wore.

"Prez, what are we supposed to do with her?"

"I told you to kill her. That piece of shit, Priest, beat the hell out of my nephew. I can't let that stand. Those Steel Order motherfuckers need to stay the fuck out our business. Those girls were going to bring us so much money, and they ruined everything. We can't even try to get new girls because the police are onto us now!"

"What's their problem anyway?" one of the other men asks. "It's not like they don't move drugs and weapons either. What's it matter if we take a couple of girls no one cares about?"

The lack of remorse in their voices makes me want to climb to my feet and punch the men in their noses, but with my feet and hands bound and my head still swimming, I can't exactly leave the floor.

"Ever since Priest took over, they've been going more and more legit. Now, those fuckers are always meddling in—"

My head whips up when I catch the distant rumble of motorcycles growing louder and louder by the second. The sound reverberates through the walls of the warehouse, sending shivers down my spine.

"Fuck!" one of the men curses. "Do you think that's our crew?" His voice is shaky, indicating he doesn't believe that himself.

I can feel their anxiety build as the noise intensifies then cuts off completely. The sudden silence is deafening, and the men don't move. Finally, the one they'd called Prez walks toward the front windows, but he doesn't make it far before the doors burst open and a bunch of armed men storm in, guns ready to fire. My jaw drops to the floor at the scene, completely forgetting my headache. The pounding intensifies in my heart instead when I notice the patches on their vests.

I would know the Steel Order patch anywhere; I've spent the better part of two days looking through Priest's closet and staring at the steel, scale, and gun patch on most of his jackets.

As it turns out, I am not the only one stunned by their arrival as the three men drop to their knees, yelling for the bikers to not shoot.

"Don't shoot, please!" one of my kidnappers yells, but my attention is not on them. Instead, it's on the giant striding toward me with long, angry steps. He kicks one of the kneeling men on his way to me, and I wince at the pained cry he lets out.

Priest drops to his knee, taking out a knife from a sheath and cutting at the zip ties binding my hands and feet. He then proceeds to run his cold dark eyes over me to make sure I am not hurt.

"What do you want to do with them?" I catch Knight's cold voice from somewhere behind Priest.

"Take them to the Barn," Priest instructs.

"Figured you might say that," Knight responds. "Let's go, boys."

There is a lot of complaining and pleading from the kneeling men, but soon, everyone empties out of the warehouse, leaving Priest and I alone.

"I'm sorry, princess," he grinds out through clenched teeth. "I should have expected they would try to come after you."

"It's not your fault," I whisper, cupping my giant's face, but he seems set on beating himself up.

"No, it's entirely my fault. I should have sent a prospect along with you for protection. I will assign someone to go along with you—"

A laugh bubbles out of me, cutting off his words. It's not light or airy as it echoes through the empty warehouse with how loud it is.

A few days ago, I never imagined I would be this happy. No one makes me as happy as Priest does.

"Only you, I swear," I say happily, brushing my lips against his firmly set ones. "Only you would get someone to shadow me taking classes." It's ridiculous, but it leaves me giddy that he would do something like that.

"I would do anything for you, princess."

"I see that," I whisper, brushing my lips along his once more, desire pushing out the anxiety that'd rocked me before.

He's here. I'm safe now.

Priest grabs my chin and tips it up as he gives into my need, kissing me and slowly draining the tension from my body. I wrap my arms around his shoulders even as I open up for him, our tongues dragging together in wet friction..

It has to be bad to feel so good. Every moment with this man tops the last in ways I could never have expected.

A sigh escapes my lips as I slip my hand under his vest to feel his chiseled muscles move under my fingers and love every second of it.

"We need to get you out of here, sweetheart," Priest rasps between kisses, but he's already dragging his hand up my skirt, leaving a trail of heat in every spot his fingers graze. "We can't stay in enemy territory for long."

"We'll be fast," I whimper against his lips, pushing up and practically climbing into his lap. My panties are damp with arousal, and the need for him grows by the second. I need to feel him inside me, but more than that . . . I want to reward him for coming to my rescue not once, but twice.

He brought dozens of his men just to rescue me.

My Daddy deserves to be rewarded for keeping his promise to protect me. To be reminded that I am the lucky one.

"Fuck, princess, what are you doing to me?" he hisses when I slip my hand between us and start working on his pants. My breathing grows short when I wrap my hand around his thick length, jerking him even as I tilt my head back when his lips drop to my neck.

I'm whimpering his name when he leans in to drag his tongue over my throat, my sex dripping with need, the feeling growing more intense with every kiss. "Want you, Daddy," I whimper, tugging hard at his swollen cock. He must share the sentiment because he reaches under my skirt and pushes my panties aside.

"I'm going to fuck you, princess. So fucking hard, you'll still be feeling me every time you sit down."

Oh God!

"Yes, Daddy," I sob, scrambling to position myself over him and guiding his thick, swollen cock to my pulsing heat. I'm dripping and needy, my body practically vibrating with the need for him as he fills me with every last inch of his massive shaft. His hand slips under my thigh to my ass as he rolls his hips. I'm already moving over him when he starts rocking into me, slowly at first before he picks up pace, fucking me harder, lifting me with both hands under my thighs and pulling me roughly back down so I'm impaled on his cock over and over again.

"So fucking tight!" he chokes. "How are you still so fucking tight, princess? And choking my cock with your wet little cunt."

My back arches and my head falls back as he drives his manhood into me, sending a rush of heat to my core and a tremble to my heart. It's too much, and yet, not enough.

"Harder, Daddy," I sob, feeling myself draw closer and closer to the edge, craving that free-falling feeling that only he can give me.

Priest gives into my desire, ramming into my sex like a crazed man, and when he molds his mouth with mine to capture my cry, I give in. It's more a touch of skin with our breaths mingling hot against each other than it is a kiss but . . . it's perfect.

Everything about this man is perfect.

"Touch yourself, princess," he growls against my lips. "Do it how Daddy showed you."

I nod frantically, dipping my hand between us to rub at the tight bundles of nerves, the friction of my fingers against my clit sending me over the edge with little warning as the explosion breaks through, sending stars shooting behind my eyes as my sex cinches hard around his wide girth. He's an animal, so feral as he pounds into me until he follows me off the cliff.

"Fuck!" he roars, his muscles bunching a second before I feel him spill his warm seed into my wet heat, rocking his hips faster and harder into me until I am a broken, sobbing mess in his lap. "Fuck, princess. I love you. *You're everything to me,*" he breathes roughly into my ear.

He's everything to me, too.

Before him and the Steel Order MC, I had no one. Just a lost girl wandering a strange city for anyone to take advantage of, and he saved me.

He became my world too, and perhaps if my heart wasn't pounding in my ears and I wasn't gasping for air, I would tell him that. Instead, I settle for wrapping my arms around him, burying my face in his neck, and making a silent wish to the stars for a future with this man.

A happy, loving future with my gentle giant.

Epilogue

Two Years Later

Priest

The blindfold was a bad idea.

Guiding a man my size through a field of rocks and twigs is never a good idea, but I am a man in love and would do anything the love of my life asks of me. Hell, I know I would walk into a burning flame if she wanted me to.

"Can you please trust me? I'm not going to let you fall." My wife's enchanting voice distracts me from the disaster that is waiting to happen. Her siren call is a soft melody that dances in the air, filling my heart with warmth and love. When she laughs, it's bright and airy, filled with so much tenderness, it makes me fall even deeper in love with her, something I never thought could happen.

"Princess . . ."

"We're almost there," she whispers giddily, her pure joy transferring to me, and I find myself smiling too. I have been doing a lot of that lately.

"We've been walking for an hour."

"You are just being dramatic. It hasn't even been ten minutes," she scolds. "How is it I never noticed how impatient you are?"

Because we did everything backward. Unlike most people who date then get married, Sky and I did the opposite. We got married first and then slowly learned the other's unique quirks. Like her little habit of rearranging the furniture in the middle of the night when she can't sleep. It wasn't until I stubbed my toe on the way to get a glass of water one night that I made it a habit not to walk in the dark around the house. Or even more charming, the way she used to trade the cigarettes in my jacket pockets for snacks or lip balm or any number of random trinkets.

I choke back a laugh at the memory of the one time during an operation to catch the cop who'd been working with the traffickers, I reached into my jacket for my cigarettes only to find them replaced with a tube of shiny pink lip gloss. Knight had looked over right at that moment and let me know that rose wasn't really my color. He still hasn't let me live it down. The message to quit smoking was clear. Suffice it to say, I never touched another cigarette from that day.

The memory of finally catching the motherfucker that was taking advantage of his position in the community as a police officer who could be trusted and facilitating the kidnapping of vulnerable girls is still fresh in my mind. My brothers had a field day working on him in the Barn before we finally released them to our contact on the force with enough evidence to put him away.

It's been two years since then. The Steel Order MC sponsored the construction of a women's shelter dedicated to being a safe haven for women and girls with no place else to go. We make sure everyone knows the place is under our protection and that anyone who touches the vulnerable people at the shelter would be answering to us.

The Black Chains are also no more. After their president orchestrated Sky's kidnapping as payback for me beating his nephew and disrupting his trafficking ring, I made sure he'd never again be a problem. We absorbed all of their businesses and territory, along with most of their members. Anyone who wanted to join our MC was welcome, as long as they agreed to play by our rules. Those who had a role in Sky's kidnapping or the human trafficking ring were given the same level of mercy they'd shown the young women they'd kidnapped.

"We're here!" Sky beams, her voice drawing me back to the present. She tugs the blindfold off my face, and when my eyes lock on her clear blues, I am hypnotized, sucked back into her web.

"How did I land someone as beautiful and gorgeous as you?" I rasp, watching with satisfaction as her cheeks flush a pretty rosy hue. She brushes her hair behind her ear before looking away, but I don't miss the shy smile that grazes her lips.

"Stop looking at me and focus on the present I worked so hard on."

My eyes shift from her and sweep around the place my wife has brought me. The slight tension in me eases when I realize we're still on the private land of the Steel Order's clubhouse. The spot is secluded, ringed by trees that often act as a natural cover to our land.

The spot we're standing on is surrounded by tall swaying grass and wildflowers. In the middle, there's a cozy picnic blanket laid out with a large picnic basket sitting in its center with a small box next to it. The gentle breeze carries the scents of nature, mingling with the delicious aroma of brewed coffee.

The only sounds I hear are the rustling leaves and the distant chirping of birds. It's just us, I realize, intimately surrounded by nature.

"How did you get everything down here?" I ask, marveling at her hard work, but my eyes are focused on the box next to the basket seated in the middle of the spread blanket. A part of me suspects what lies inside, but I say nothing, unwilling to ruin her surprise.

"I found prospects to help me carry everything with the promise to let them ride your bike later."

My head spins to her so fast, I almost give myself whiplash, but the tension dissipates when I am met by her laughing face. "Oh my God, you should have seen your face." She doubles over with laughter.

"That is not funny."

"It was. Just a little," she chuckles, clutching her stomach as her body shakes with laughter. "No, I just promised to introduce them to some of my single friends from my college." I shake my head, nodding at the small box seated on the ground, and she jumps up, grabs my hand, and pulls me down on the blanket before reaching for the box. "I have an even bigger surprise for you."

"What is it?" I ask, tugging at the wrapping to see what's inside. I pull out a neatly folded piece of paper and read through it.

"I'm pregnant," she says excitedly. "I just found out yesterday, and I've been holding it in. I was thinking, I'll take a break from college after I have the baby, maybe take some of my classes from home, and . . ."

Her voice trails off, and the smile on her face falls when her eyes connect with mine.

"What?" I ask, my brows drawn in confusion.

"You don't look surprised by the news," she says. "You knew?"

Fuck, I must not have the best poker face when it comes to her.

"I did," I say, dropping the box to pull her onto my lap. "I was waiting for you to tell me."

"But how . . . how did you find out before me?"

"Because I know you," I whisper, brushing my finger over her jaw and down her chest. "Your boobs have been tender and swollen lately, more sensitive when I touch you." Her cheeks flame, but I don't let her look away, cupping her breasts over her dress, and true to my words, she lets out a shudder, her nipples pebbling and pushing hard against the material. "You've definitely become hornier than ever before. Haven't you noticed how often we have sex lately, with you waking me up at odd hours of the night to ride my dick? Yesterday, you made me stop my bike in the middle of the road for sex."

"Oh, God!" she cries, covering her face with the palms of her hands.

"I don't even have to touch you to get you all slicked up for my cock. You're always so wet."

"Stop talking, please," she begs, but she's leaning into my touch when I snake my hand under her dress and yank her panties down her thighs. Her lips part on a gasp when I tear her panties off and toss them over my shoulder.

"Fine, let me show you then," I say, rubbing my middle finger over her damp folds, her sex already slick and trembling when I push my thick digit into her. I let out a groan when her walls lock tightly around my finger, pulsing needily around it. "Fuck, baby. Look how tight and needy you are for me."

Her eyes lock with mine, and there is so much desire in those perfect blues, for a second, I lose myself in them. Her hips start moving, rocking slowly over my thick digit, the wet heat around my digit sending my cock leaking with the need to replace it.

"Oh, Daddy. Need you now," she whimpers, her breathing growing more labored by the second and hips moving feverishly over mine.

"Fuck, I need to be inside you now, princess," I say harshly, drawing my finger out of her to work on my zipper. My cock is swollen and throbbing hard when I finally lay her back on the blanket and guide my heavy shaft into her sex, driving hard into her tight wet pussy, her moan mingling with my deep groan.

"Ah, harder, Daddy!"

I wrap my arm under her thigh and lift it to my hip before driving into her pulsing heat with a heavy grunt. The way our bodies move together, from the slap of our connecting flesh to the beautiful sounds she makes, draws me deeper into her web.

Two years of loving this woman, and I am as obsessed with her as I was the first day I met her, if not more. I thought putting a ring on her finger would rein in the possessive bastard in me, but all it's done is make things worse.

I'm addicted to this girl.

I don't see that changing any time soon. Ever.

"Mine!" I growl as I pound into her harder, drinking up her broken cries and flushed face. My lovely wife—and soon, the mother of my children. She is so fucking perfect and all mine!

"So close, Daddy," she sobs, thrashing fervently when I reach between us to pet her swollen clit with my thumb, the slippery friction sending her over the edge with a scream that no doubt scares the birds from the trees close by.

I swallow her cries when I press my lips to hers just as my balls erupt, and everything around us blurs as I spill my seed into her. "I love you, princess," I breathe against her lips, rocking my cock into her as she milks me with her pulsing sex.

"God, you're right," she heaves, wrapping her arms weakly around my shoulders when I drop down on top of her. "I can't believe I didn't realize just how much I've grown to crave this. I still . . ."

I push up a bit to meet her eyes, mirth no doubt dancing in mine. "You want to go again?"

Her cheeks and neck flush a deeper shade of red as she looks away, but I can read the truth in her eyes. I could get used to my insatiable little wife—a challenge I fully accept.

"Maybe," she says with a giggle, offering her lips for a kiss, and I am too weak to resist. To everyone else, I am the dangerous president of the largest and most powerful motorcycle club in Austin, but to Sky, I am simply a man smitten with his wife.

I wouldn't want it any other way.

~The End

More Books By Cassi

Tempting My Stepbrother

Tempting the Doctor

Stalked Series:

Soulmate Stalker

My Modern Viking Stalker

My Secret Santa My Stalker

Overprotective Stalker

Seeing Double Twin Sister Series:

Fake Athlete

The Professor's Copy

Pretend Ring Girl

Fake Assistant

Standalones:

His Runaway Valentine

Dirty Puck: F*** On the Ice Rink

Zorion: Demonic Disciples

Bred by the Boss

Vowed to be Yours

Sold To The Biker

Happily Ever After Mountain:

The Loner's Prize

Beauty and the Recluse

Chasing Glass Slippers

The Billionaire's Final Treasure

Courting Curves:

Defending Her Heart

Sweetheart Campus:

Coaches Pet

Hot for Professor

Tutoring the Athlete

The Dean's Daughter

Boxsets:

Sweet Obsessions Boxset: Suddenly His Series Collection

His Obsession: A Stalker Collection

Seeing Double: Sister Swap Collection

Extra Credit Collection: Sweetheart Campus

Glamorous Brides Collection

Happily Ever After Collection

Emerald City Billionaire's

Steel Order MC

Be Mine: Valentine's Collection

Feel the Love

Big Alpha's:

Big Brawny Mechanic

Big Hulking Biker

Big Bold Security

Big Beefy Kingpin

Glamorous Brides:

Cuffing His Bride

The Hitman's Bride

Farmer Finds a Bride

Doctor's Surprise Bride

The BFF Pact:

His Weakness

His Mistake

His Apprentice

His Promise

Dearly Devoted:

Stalked by the Convict

Stepbrother's Little Secret

Stalked by the Marine

Hacking my Stalker

Stalked by the Mobster

Saved by my Stalker

A Big Burly Romance:

Big Burly Forman (FREE book)

Big Forbidden Blacksmith

Big Brutal Roughneck

Big Grumpy Fireman

Big Merry Miner

Big Hefty Trucker

Mistletoe Love Series:

Joy for the Scrooge

Highest Bidder Club:

Auctioned to my Boss

Auctioned to my Best Friend

Auctioned to the Stranger

Auctioned to the Billionaire

The Matchmaker

Forbidden Match

Taming the Boss Series

The Grump's Fake Wife

The Tyrant's Fake Fiancé

His Toughest Case

High Stakes Deal

Rescued By Love

Her Reluctant Titan

Someone to Fight For Series

Her Cage Fighter

The Devil's Angel

The Rogue's Princess

The Viking's Kitten

Her Devoted Warrior

Her Twisted Protector

Steel Order MC Series:

Claimed By Priest

Knight's Last Chance

Mercy For Reaper

Cash's Treasure

Taming Riot

Sunshine For Shadow

Emerald City Billionaire's:

Cold Hearted Baron

Protective Boss

Blackmailing the Mogul

The Tycoon's Pet

The Billionaire's Gamble

Dedicated Billionaire

Daddy's Good Girl:

Acting For Daddy

Sweetheart Falls:

Scarred Mountain Man

Bringing Home Trouble:

One Twisted Christmas

Sold To The Naughty List:

Auctioned To The Mobster

Men Of Valor Springs:

Saved By The Mechanic

Defensive Hero

The Mobster's Flower

Dangerous Obsession

The Marine's Purpose

His Secret Addiction

Claimed By My Best Friend

Bride For The Rancher

Guarding His Sunshine

The Driver's Prize

Whiskey Mountain:

Damaged Mountain Man

Protected by the Mountain Man

Praised by the Mountain Man

Devotion by the Mountain Man

High Rollers Club:

Sold to the Titan

Sold to the Investor

Sold to the Beret

Sold to the Fighter

Sold to the Mogul

Bought by the Owner's Son

About the Author

Cassi lives to write brazen OTT, insta-love, short stories, about possessive alphas and the women they love. Stories that will leave you satisfied, and maybe blushing a little. Cassi loves pedicures, being pampered in any way possible, her darling golden Princess, amazing coffee, and traveling too anywhere warm.

Printed in Dunstable, United Kingdom